Greenwoman

A Literary Garden of . . .

Fiction ❋ Nonfiction ❋ Poetry ❋ Commentary
Biography ❋ Art ❋ Comics

Volume 5 - Ruth Stout

Editor-In-Chief: Sandra Knauf
Deputy Editor: Zora Knauf
Copy Editor and Advisor: Cheri Colburn
Chief Designer: Sandra Knauf
Web Designer/Tech. Support: Paul Spielman

Advertising contact: Sandra Knauf
(719) 473-9237
sandra@greenwomanmagazine.com

To purchase subscriptions, single copies,
and digital editions online:
www.greenwomanmagazine.com

Retailers: For more information about selling
this marvelous magazine in your store call
719-473-9237 or write
sandra@greenwomanmagazine.com

ISBN-10: 0989705684
ISBN-13: 978-0-9897056-8-4

www.greenwomanmagazine.com
www.florasforum.com
www.zeraandthegreenman.com
www.greenwomanpublishing.com
www.gardenshorts.com

Send comments, questions,
concerns, and brilliant submissions
of art and writing to:
Greenwoman Magazine, PO Box 6587,
Colorado Springs, CO 80934-6587

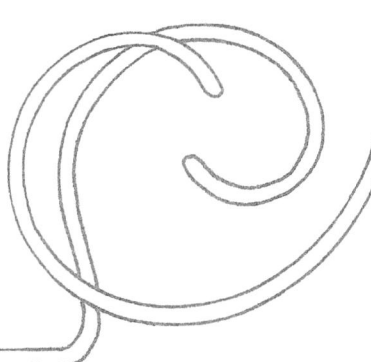

Contents

Cover art by Nadine Sage.

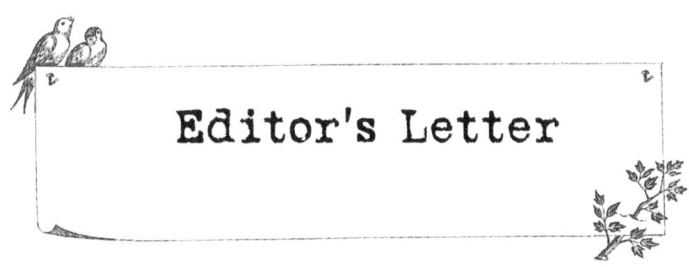

Editor's Letter

It's amazing what I see in the green community. New businesses, self-published books, charitable enterprises. In my city, among other projects, is a restaurant featuring organic, locally-grown food that allows people to pay what they can afford. All this in probably the most difficult economic time we've experienced in our lives! We're hitching up our britches, re-thinking the American dream, and beginning to create a much better one. I love it.

Two changes in this volume. First, something struck me during a recent marketing webinar. The speaker, Guy Ka-waski, referred to self-publishing as "artisanal publishing." Why not? Kawaski asked; after all, it's perfectly acceptable to have an artisanal bakery, a micro-brewery, or a charming little farm where you sell heirloom organic vegetables. Those things, in fact, are lauded. But when someone self-publishes, well, that's often different. Yes, sometimes the work is poor in quality. (Okay, the majority of work is poor in quality.) Still, the cream rises to the top. There are many who consider this work our calling. We have spent years, if not decades, mastering the craft. Kawaski inspired me to add "Artisanal Publishing" to the cover. It had a sweet ring to it, and it made me think not only of all the hard-working writers and artists who contribute to this magazine but all those who are out there elsewhere self-publishing good works.

The second change is actually the debut of a logo for Greenwoman Publishing, LLC. (See masthead and page 61.) This image was inspired by a few antique drawings of the legendary Picts, the Celts who painted their bodies before go-ing into battle. The warrior-soul, the natural/celestial designs, the beautiful ferocity: all of it resonated with me. I thought, now *here* was a female who could represent *Greenwoman*! Thank you, Mike Beenenga, for designing her, a powerful and distinctive logo for our business.

In this volume, I am also proud to introduce a new comic by talented Chicagoan Sharon Rosenzweig. It's the first in a series about illegal chicken raising in her city. The inaugural story is about the artist's mother. In this issue I am also offering a mini-biography of my earliest gardening heroine, Ruth Stout. Finally, as the icing on the cake, we were able to interview Amanda Thomsen for this issue. She is an up-and-coming garden guru, and a style-setter. When I write "up and coming," I really mean that Amanda is an artisan that has spent years mastering *her* craft and is now finally getting the attention she deserves.

You may notice that this volume contains a full-page ad (back cover) for the novel, *Zera and the Green Man*. This story has been one of my side passions/projects for over 13 years. It's a young adult sci-fi/environmental fantasy that I'm hoping will have wide-audience appeal. It's about GMOs and biotechnology, it's about the legend of the "Green Man" —but mostly it's a story about family, and love—because, really, isn't that all that matters? It is available on Amazon in print and as an e-book. I would be honored if you would read my first novel and let me know what you think! Better yet, leave a review on Amazon and help spread the word.

Sandra

Sandra Knauf
Editor and Publisher

Contributors

Born in Rochester, New York, **Laura Chilson** graduated with her BFA from SUNY Purchase School of Art+Design in 2008. She currently resides in Ithaca, NY. She specializes in pencil portraits and oil paintings and can be reached through her website, www.LauraChilson.com.

Coloradoan **James A. Ciletti** has been the Pikes Peak Poet Laureate, the president of Poetry West, and is co-owner of the independent bookstore Hooked on Books. Ciletti has published two books of poetry, won numerous awards for his work, and has debuted the first chapter of his upcoming novel in a writing magazine. He also teaches creative writing classes at the Fremont Correctional Facility.

Cheryl Conklin, also from Colorado, is a landscape gardener, writer, and educator lucky enough to have followed her bliss. You can see more of her work, find contact information, and link to her blog, *Gardenhood*, at www.greenwaygardening.com

Barbara Crooker's work has been read many times by Garrison Keillor on *The Writer's Almanac*. Her books are *Radiance* (Word Press), *Line Dance* (Word Press), *More* (C&R Press), and *Gold* (Cascade Books). She lives and gardens in rural northeastern Pennsylvania, where two burning bushes grace her front landscaping.

Rachael Davis says, "I consider it fate when I met [editor] Sandra at a start-up meeting for a downtown organic and local farmer's market." They've been collaborating and swapping stories on gardening adventures, children, and creative work ever since. Rachael's mixed media art has been shown in Colorado. She holds a BFA from the Kansas City Art Institute and is now pursuing a MFA in Fort Collins, Colorado.

Kathryn Eastburn was co-founder and editor of the *Colorado Springs Independent*, where her work garnered numerous awards. Other work has appeared in publications across the U.S., including the *Denver Post*, *Saveur*, and *Texas Highways*, and she has published two books of literary nonfiction. Currently she is visiting professor of Creative Nonfiction Writing and Journalism at The Colorado College, and a faculty member at Denver's Lighthouse Writers Workshop. Her radio column, *The Middle Distance*, is broadcast Saturdays on KRCC-FM, 91.5, Colorado Springs.

Pat Cook Gulya enjoys the Colorado outdoors through biking and hiking, and attempting to capture such experiences through words. She teaches and practices yoga, and thanks to a technology career retirement, has the luxury of living rather than worrying about making a living. She no longer resides at the orchard house in the country but tends a variety of garden, yard, and house plants in her urban home.

Contributors

Sheryl Humphrey is an artist in Staten Island, NY. Her paintings are often inspired by beautiful, strange myths about plants and the forces of Nature. In 2012, she self-published *The Haunted Garden: Death and Transfiguration in the Folklore of Plants*.
See her art at sherylhumphrey.tumblr.com.

Elisabeth Kinsey teaches writing online, lives in Denver, pines away for Half Moon Bay, and publishes in *The Denver Post* and various journals. Her hands are imminently dirty. She may or may not be related to the late Dr. Alfred Kinsey.

Leslie Macon is an oil painter living and working in Archer Lodge, North Carolina. She started as a wood carver (fashioning decoy ducks from basswood and tupelo) and switched to wildlife painting in the early 90s. After winning some awards, she began experimenting with floral and still life, and later branched out into historic portraits and visionary/fantasy art. She has had several collections published for the home décor market and some of her art has been made into licensed products. Visit her gallery at www.dailypaintworks.com/Artists/leslie-macon-3251.

Dan Murphy is a seasoned zine writer (*The Juniper*, *Elephant Mess*) and proponent of the slow life. His long-time passions include bike riding, skateboarding, punk rock, and gardening. His new interests include botany, ecology, wildflowers, and lichens. Dan has a B.S. in horticulture and an M.S. in biology (his thesis was on green roof technology research). He works at the Idaho Botanical Garden in Native Plant Horticulture. Learn more about Dan at www.juniperbug.blogspot.com

Michelle Ayn Potter is a writer, photographer, and gardener who finds great inspiration and creativity in the nature around us. She writes a blog, *The Sage Butterfly*, and has written several books, the latest being *150 Things You Can Compost*. She has won awards for her photography and poetry and had her work published in books and magazines. Her web site is www.michelleaynpotter.com.

Will Raap, founder of the Intervale Center, Restoring Our Watershed and Gardener's Supply, is engaged in creating positive social, environmental and economic change by employing the power of markets and social enterprises. He focuses on local food, renewable energy, and land restoration enterprises that support a more resilient economy and more sustainable future. Other initiatives include The Earth Partners, Reforest Teak, Farm at South Village and the New Economics Institute.

Bruce Holland Rogers was born in dry, dry Tucson, Arizona, and now lives in wet, wet Eugene, Oregon. He enjoys the prospect of gardening but doesn't much like the actual work. Rogers teaches fiction writing in the MFA program of the Northwest Institute of Literary Arts.
www.shortshortshort.com

Contributors

Investigative cartoonist **Sharon Rosenzweig** is passionate about backyard chickens. Fowl are outlawed in her town, so the home poultry movement has gone undercoop. Rosenzweig seeks out tales of forbidden flocks and leads readers into the netherworld of hidden hens and renegade eggs.

DB Rudin is an environmental education consultant, elementary school teacher, and the Education Coordinator at Venetucci Farm, an 190-acre historic farm in Colorado Springs, Colorado. He offers programs through Colorado Critter Encounters, which includes hands-on programs for kids on nature and conservation, and a class for those who tend the soil, The Good, the Bad and the Beautiful: Bugs 101 for Gardeners. www.cocritterencounters.com

Nadine Sage (whose work again graces this issue's cover) is a papier collé and oil artist. Encouraging a renewed appreciation for master illustrators of the past, Nadine infuses the past with the present. She integrates 18th and 19th century illustrations and imagery with contemporary decorative components. Collage never looked so good. www.nadinesage.com

Rob Schultz taught American literature at Western Michigan University and Virginia Commonwealth University before drifting into radio and voice work. He has published a first novel, *Styll in Love*. Meanwhile, another novel, "On-Air," seeks a publisher. Stories and poems have appeared or are forthcoming in over two dozen publications, including *Euphony*, *New Plains Review*, *Prime Mincer*, and *Bluestem Magazine*. He and his wife, Aletha, live in Richmond, Virginia.

"Gardening," Thomas Rowlandson, (1756-1827), via Wikimedia Commons

Gardening with a Purpose

Out on the bike path, I took the earphones out of my ears for once. The sounds I heard were suddenly beautiful, regardless how mind-numbingly mundane they often are. Bits of conversations from passing trail users entered my ears, along with the rushing of an adjacent river and the chirping of birds. The roaring of cars on nearby roads was even welcome, simply due to how unfamiliar it seemed. Usually, I have music blasting to block it all out. Listening to it all un-muted made me wonder what I have been missing all this time.

As I ride, I recognize that I am riding in concert with other bike enthusiasts and I am sharing the trail with people who value the unique beauty of the outdoor world. Certainly some may be more passionate about this than others, but it occurs to me that even though nature's offerings may so frequently be taken for granted, they are utilized by all of us. Yet the list of environmental challenges unique to our time continues to grow, threatening our very way of life. Preserving what is left of our natural environment then becomes paramount in order to maintain the health of the complex processes that breathe life into this planet and afford us the opportunity to enjoy the short time we have here.

This is why I choose to garden with a purpose. I don't want to lose what I take for granted or be responsible for anyone else's loss, whether now or in the future. I realize that life is a blur and that there are often too many other things occupying our time that it becomes difficult to be concerned about issues outside of ourselves, but we must. And luckily, it may only take minor adjustments in our lifestyles to make huge differences in the long run. Adjusting our approach to gardening is one big step in the right direction.

by
Dan Murphy

A rain garden, when constructed properly, collects runoff during a storm and holds it in place, keeping it from rushing into storm drains and then out into waterways where it can disrupt fragile ecosystems or cause major flooding. A rain garden can also filter out pollutants and impurities while simultaneously aiding in groundwater recharge. Green roofs and bioswales offer similar benefits, and a green roof has the added benefit of lowering the inside temperatures of a building, reducing our energy use.

A xeriscape garden reduces water use. Fresh water is a valuable and increasingly scarce resource, so lessening the need for irrigation in a landscape becomes imperative when all the other myriad needs for fresh water are considered. And being water-wise doesn't have to mean sacrificing aesthetics either, despite what the critics say. Growing numbers of beautifully designed xeric gardens are continuing to prove otherwise.

A gardener is the ideal person to help reintroduce habitat for native wildlife. Designing and planting gardens that feed and provide habitat for native insects, birds, and other creatures, helps to ensure that local ecosystems remain intact. Forbs, grasses, shrubs, and trees that are native to a specific region are ideal plants to have in a landscape in order to attract, feed, and house native animal species. This is especially important for migrating insects and birds, because they often rely on certain food sources along their course of travel and during their relatively short life cycles. Butterfly gardens and other wildlife friendly plantings are great examples of gardening with a purpose.

Of course, we humans have to eat too, so any garden that includes edible plants also serves a greater purpose. Choosing to include in our yards food producing plants means that searching elsewhere for food becomes less of a requirement. The number of miles your food must travel to get to you becomes zero when you can walk out your door and pick it yourself. Not only is the pollution caused by food transport reduced, but the level of agricultural chemicals also decreases when people chose instead to produce their own food and refrain from purchasing the typical produce section fare.

I realize that purposeful gardening may be an ambiguous concept. What is the purpose, and who gets to decide what is purposeful and what is not? Doesn't a well-designed and well-manicured garden full of attractive and interesting, exotic plant species serve some kind of purpose? Of course it does. As a devout gardener and full-fledged plant nerd, I am not willing to discard.

the fact that a garden of any kind or style can be amazing, and, in fact, psychologically rewarding (a purpose in its own right). However, the planet is small, and our time on it is short, and there are things here worth looking after and preserving. Humans, with their advanced and extraordinary ability to look into the future and comprehend the potential results of our oftentimes careless and shortsighted actions, are faced with the obligation to act responsibly. Gardeners are in an excellent position to incorporate a certain level of responsibility into their craft. The question then becomes, will we continue to take for granted the unique beauty of this planet (regardless how mundane it can seem at times) or will we move forward with purpose, addressing the challenges at hand one plant at a time? ❀

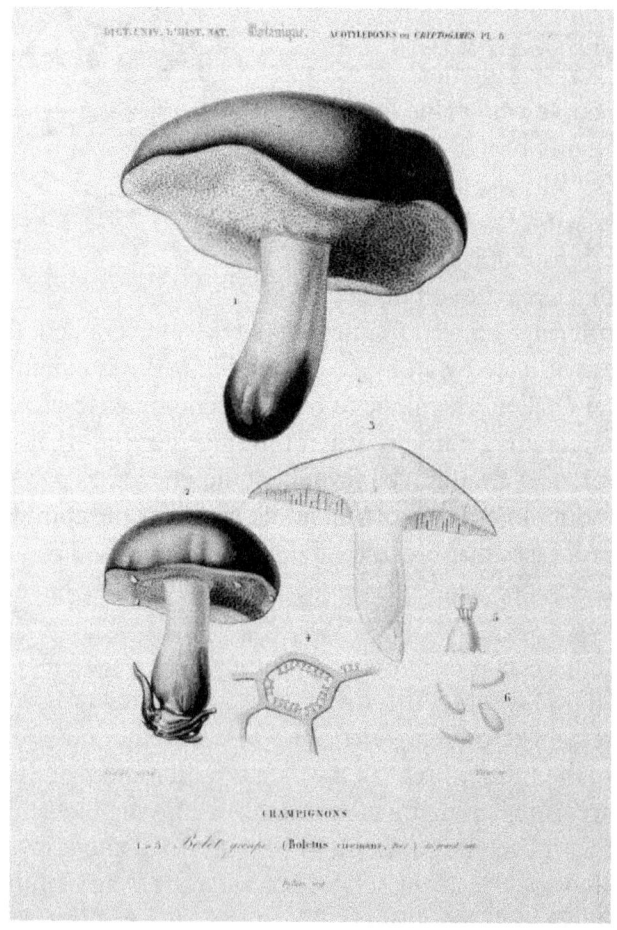

"Champignons" (*Boletus circinans*), 1849
MM Renard, Martinet Et C

Wild Bee, I Think I Love You

by Will Raap

Honey bees and wild pollinators need your help and need it now.

Gardeners know that good pollination makes for better crops of tomatoes, cucumbers, apples, and raspberries. And that's especially true for certain commercial crops like almonds, which need to have one million honeybee hives brought to California's Central Valley to provide pollination for 60 million trees, supporting 80% of the world's almond production. But wild bees, beetles, flies, butterflies, moths, birds, and bats also are critical in moving pollen from the male to the female parts of flowers for fruit and seed setting.

The journal *Science* affirmed this point with a recently published study of 600 sites in 20 countries involving 41 crops. It found that wild insects are more important than we may have thought for crop pollination and that honeybees cannot replace the value and importance of wild pollinators. *Science* reported that "Wild insects pollinated crops more effectively, because an increase in their visitation enhanced fruit set by twice as much as an equivalent increase in honeybee visitation. Further, visitation by wild insects and honeybees promoted fruit set independently, so high abundance of managed honey bees supplemented, rather than substituted for, pollination by wild insects."

So our gardens and farms need BOTH wild insect and honey bee pollinators.

What can be done?

Wild pollinators usually live in natural habitats, such as the edges of forests, wetlands,

Jaime Zuñiga Leal (right), ROW's first Bees for Trees producer, received beekeeping training in 2011, when he and his wife received a loan for 15 hives. They'll repay their loan this year, and be given a second loan to add 25 more hives to their farm. www.ourwatershed.org/projects/bees-for-trees-project

and riparian zones, hedgerows or grasslands. The *Science* article shows agriculture can also help promote nature's free pollinator services with practices that conserve or restore natural areas around and within croplands, add diverse flowering plants, provide nesting areas, and minimize and/or ban pesticide use. Sure, farmers with flowering crops can always pay to bring in commercial honeybee hives, but it may be cheaper and will be more effective and better for the environment if we design farming systems to help wild pollinators thrive.

I helped created a non-profit program, Bees for Trees, that is helping families in Costa Rica become beekeepers. It provides participating families with a zero-interest micro-loan to begin producing honey from 10 hives—enough to increase household income by 30 to 50 percent. In return, these small landowners must stop using toxic pesticides and herbicides and also reforest 10% of their denuded land, thus reducing erosion, increasing groundwater reserves, and improving wild pollinator habitat. We're working on a crowd-sourcing campaign, where a $25 donation can help us expand the program and get you some fresh Costa Rican honey.

The *Science* article concluded that without steps to conserve wild pollinators, "The ongoing loss of wild insects is destined to compromise agricultural yields worldwide."

What if every farmer, large and small, were supported to be good stewards of the nature around them by being offered incentives that improve their overall income, not just financial but also the kinds that healthy ecosystems offer for free? ✳

Tomato Love

by
James A. Ciletti

One skin-tight bite
of this sweet tarty tomato
cancels all dominion of the self.

Tasting the flesh in this flesh
one easily becomes translucent.
Criss-crossing the tomato heart,
brigades of sensations sensate my mouth.

So what's this shake-out between
eating tomatoes and making love?
This skin blushing red to a simple touch,
this full fleshy feeling plump in the hand,
aroma divine of the love apple from the vine,
the skin kissable above or below the nipple or navel?

For what's a kiss on the cheek, or luscious red lips,
but the flesh of a tomato ripe in the mouth.
Ah! To live where tomatoes ripen every day!
Every hour! Now! Taste the tarty tomato.

A Life of the Mind

By Bruce Holland Rogers

My ex-wife has come for the children. She brings her new husband along. His name is Matthew. He is smart. He talks about parts of Europe that make me want to get out a map, if I could find one. He says irredentism, and other words I do not know. He wears long sleeves and a hat, even on this July day, because he is allergic to sun.

My ex-wife has come for the children. It is her turn. Their turn, hers and Matthew's. She says Matthew lives a life of the mind. He is a good influence on the children, she says. My ex and Matthew have driven the four miles from the highway in Matthew's Prius. They had to walk the last half mile because this year I can't pay for a grader.

My ex-wife has come for the children, and the children scramble out of the house to greet her. My children know that I built this house with my own hands. They know this fact, but do they feel it in their bones? In their step-father's back yard, they have a swimming pool. Matthew, when he swims with them, swims covered up.

My ex-wife has come for the children. They are all going to fly to Croatia. I have hardly been out of the state, and last month, when my crew was idled, I had to calculate mileage to the half-gallon and price beans and rice by the meal. If anyone asked me, I would say that such calculations are living a life of the mind.

My ex-wife has come for the children, and left with them. The house, which I built with my own hands, is too quiet. I think of my children days from now, half a world away, walking on a beach in Europe. They will find things in the sand. My ex-wife's voice will sound bright and happy. Matthew will be covered up. I strip naked. I lie down in the long summer grass. Ants crawl over me. I let them. I stay there, absorbing sunlight, until I feel strong again.

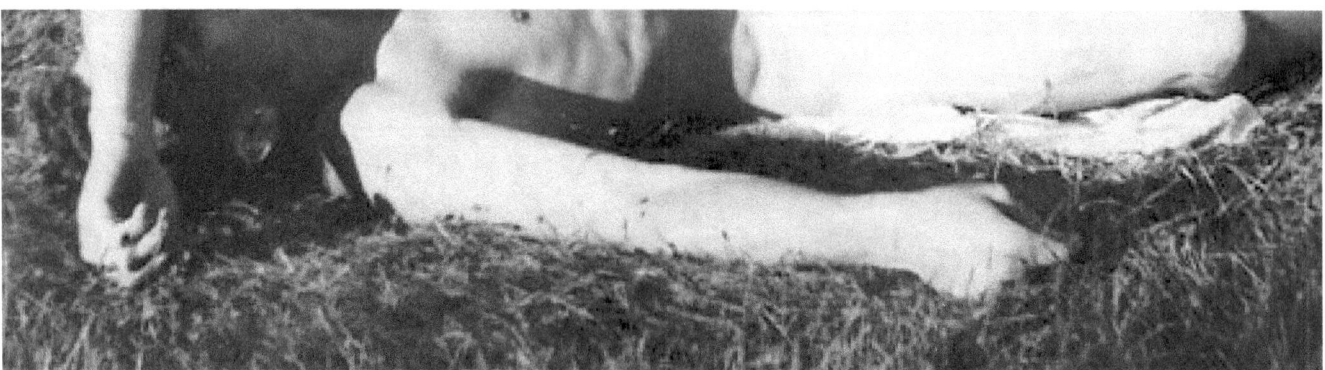

Name that Seed - Antique Edition

See how many seeds in this 1779 engraving you can identify.
(Hint: They are labeled in Dutch.)

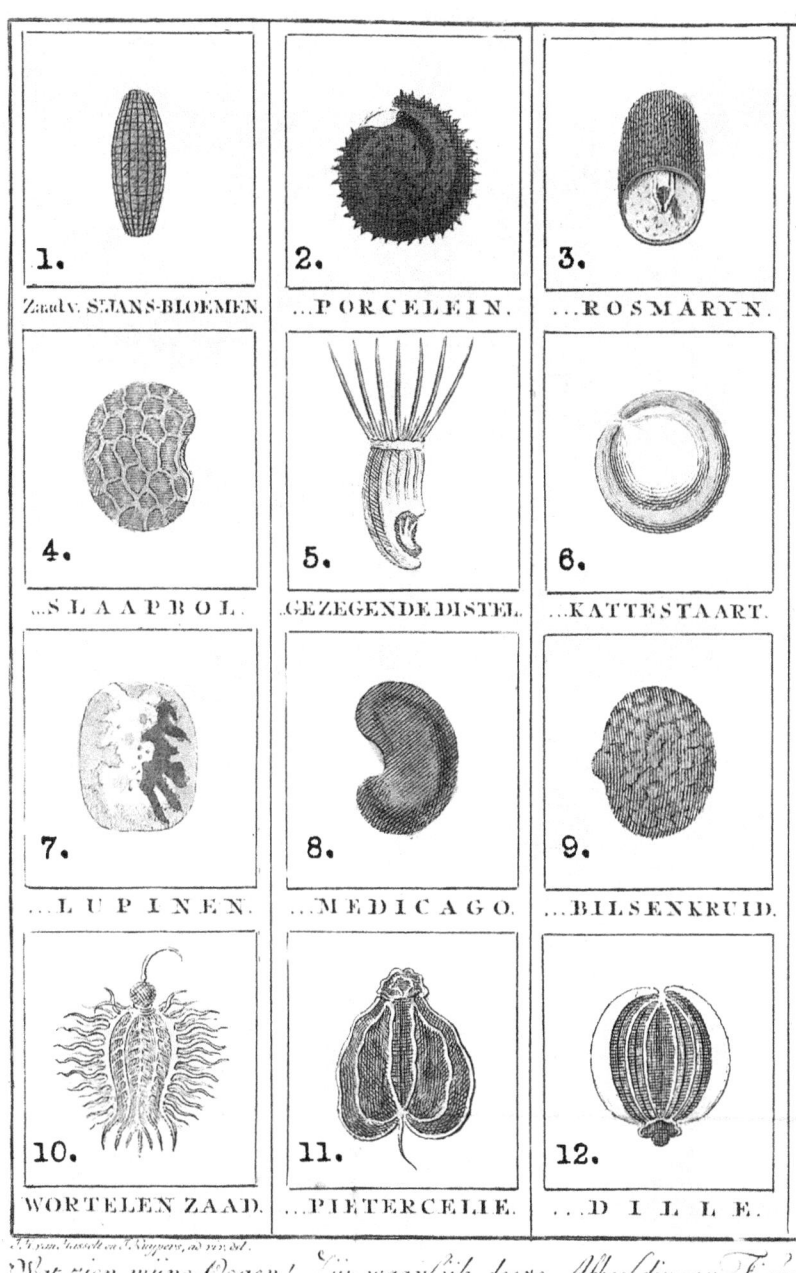

1. Zaad v. ST.JANS-BLOEMEN.	2. ...PORCELEIN.	3. ...ROSMARYN.
4. ...SLAAPBOL.	5. GEZEGENDE DISTEL.	6. ...KATTESTAART.
7. ...LUPINEN.	8. ...MEDICAGO.	9. ...BILSENKRUID.
10. WORTELEN ZAAD.	11. ...PIETERCELIE.	12. ...DILLE.

Wat zien myne Oogen! Zyn waarlyk deeze, Afbeeldingen Figu...

Answers:

1-locust flower; 2-porcelain plant; 3-rosemary; 4-breadseed poppy; 5-blessed thistle; 6-loosestrife; 7-lupin; 8-medicago; 9-black henbane; 10-carrot; 11-parsley; 12-dill.

The Pot of Basil

From *The Haunted Garden* - Giovanni Boccaccio's dark poem retold

by Sheryl Humphey

John White Alexander, *Isabella and the Pot of Basil*, (1897)

 novella from Giovanni Boccaccio's collection "The Decameron" (ca. 1350-53) was later adapted into a narrative poem by John Keats, "Isabella, or the Pot of Basil" (1818). The poem was the subject of paintings by Pre-Raphaelite artists William Holman Hunt and John Everett Millais.

The tale involves the fair young maiden Lisabetta (or Isabella) and her three brothers, wealthy merchants of Messina.

The brothers expected Isabella to marry a man suited to her high station in society, but she fell in love with handsome Lorenzo, who worked for the brothers. When the brothers discovered the relationship, they led Lorenzo to a remote place where they murdered and buried him. They told everyone, including Isabella, that they had sent Lorenzo abroad on business for them, and that he would not return for a long time.

The lovesick Isabella became more and more despairing as time passed with no word from Lorenzo. She feared that something evil had happened to him, but she knew not what. Each night she cried and called out Lorenzo's name, beseeching him to return to her.

One night, his ghost appeared to her and told her the truth of how and where he was slain by her brothers. In the morning, Isabella slipped away from the house with a trusted servant and went to the scene of the crime. Under the dead leaves, she noticed an area where the ground was soft, and began to dig. There lay the corpse of her lover, unblemished by decay. Unable to transport the body, and frantic from fear of her brothers, Isabella cut off the head from the body and took it home, where she lamented over Lorenzo's death and kissed his head a thousand times. To keep him with her, yet unseen by others, she buried the head in a large garden pot that she then planted with sweet basil.

Every day Isabella sat by the pot of basil, gazing and sighing at it longingly. Every day her grief overwhelmed her, and she wept so much that the basil was watered by her tears. The plants flourished from her attention, but she became weaker and weaker.

Her brothers eventually discovered the source of her obsession, and secretly took away the pot and buried the head. With her health and spirit broken, Isabella piteously and continuously asked for the pot of basil, until she died from grief. ✻

A New
(Garden Writing)
Sensation

Greenwoman interviews Amanda Thomsen
by Sandra Knauf

Illustration by Laura Chilson

Gardeners in the know, know Amanda Thomsen.

She's the lady with the cool blog, *Kiss My Aster!*, who also blogged for *Horticulture*, who now blogs and writes articles for *Fine Gardening*. and who has published her very first book on gardening named, you guessed it, *Kiss My Aster*, (subtitled: *A Graphic Guide to Creating a Fantastic Yard Totally Tailored to You*). Her Facebook page has thousands of "likes," and she's the creative genius behind those sexy-fun Ryan Gosling gardening memes (one of my recent favorites: *"Hey girl, I think we should start composting with worms . . . but only if you're into it . . ."*)

Thomsen is retro-chic, zany, slightly naughty, witty. Think Lucille Ball meets Dorothy Parker with a trowel.

With her star on the rise, it's not a surprise to learn she just left a large Chicago landscape architecture firm. She attributes that to "possible mid-life crisis," but I'm thinking garden celebrity/writing career trajectory. This summer she's in much-needed chill-out mode, hanging out in the home garden with beautiful just-turned-two cherub Hazel, and her dapper, supportive husband Dan. What will she come up with next? She says she'll definitely be writing and entertaining and she may start a business. As she puts it, "I just need some time to decompress from the last few years of crazy. . . But I might take on a few small gigs."

Greenwoman: My first question is how in the heck have you been able to balance all of this—writing, gardening, toddler, marriage?!?

AT: This balancing act has been tough. I literally got the okay on the book the same day I peed on a stick and found out that I was going to have a Hazelnut. From there it's been a race. At the job I just left, the hours were incredibly long and unpredictable. Seventy hours a week was not uncommon. And then it just never left my mind; it was just landscaping, but it was one of those always "on call" situations. 2013 has been pretty intense with speaking gigs, interviews, and whatever else that has come my way—Dan has been great at taking care of Hazel while I've been distracted, and it's brought them close together. Hazel goes to daycare and that's hard. But I went to daycare and look at me now. HA. I know that glorifying busy isn't a great thing, but being busy is my default setting. It actually brings me tremendous peace to always be moving forward.

Greenwoman: Let's backtrack. Who or what inspired you to become a gardener? A writer?

AT: When I was little I wanted to do three things when I grew up, 1. Be a writer, 2. recycle and 3. wear red lipstick. Happily, I have achieved these three goals. Although I always wanted to be a writer, I did ABSOLUTELY NOTHING to make that happen, growing up. No one pointed me in the right direction. I've taken a few writing classes but overall, nothing that was memorable. I have always been super creative and have just looked for ways to demonstrate that!

My parents were the prototypes for yuppies. For some reason, and I think it was my Dad's Indiana upbringing, they were SUPER into *Crockett's Victory Garden* on PBS and did, literally, everything he did. We have a 30' x 50' Victory garden each summer and I just grew up in it. They had a greenhouse added to the house, canned up everything from applesauce to giardiniera. It was a delicious way to grow up and I didn't realize that EVERYBODY didn't have that until I was, like, 20. Maybe older. I didn't realize there were jobs in gardening and horticulture.

Greenwoman: I love your style (and I'm not just talkin about the plants). Who are your style icons? Not only in gardening, but fashion, writing, film, whatever comes to mind.

AT: I'm obsessed with Betsey Johnson, Elsa Schiaparelli, old movies (preferably with Edith Head as the costumer), John Waters, David Lynch, Francesca Lia Block, Hello Kitty, Amy Sedaris, Pearl Fryar, 90s Riot Grrrls, and Frida Kahlo.

Greenwoman: You have this funny, sassy, sexy, free-spirited, curse-word-strewn, delightfully naughty blog for a few years (also titled "Kiss My Aster!"), and you're a landscaper, and suddenly you're blogging for Horticulture magazine's website (which lasted for several years) and now you blog for Fine Gardening (and write articles). I don't want to disrespect these fine publications, but, well, they can be at times just a bit, shall we say, dry. How did you get together with them?

A.T.: *Horticulture* asked me to join this contest they were having for a blogger. I did and I won. It was hard on me to blog exclusively for them and not on my personal blog at all, not even about personal stuff (I was pregnant and had shit to SAY) but that was the deal. *Fine Gardening* has been a great, laid back home for my more horty things to say. I leave the eff-bombs at the door and get my freak on over there and I've loved it. AND they've given me a chance to write articles, which is seriously one of my happiest achievements in life. Like, "Hi. I'm not all fluff and Ryan Gosling. I can talk to you about biennials like a badass."

All these magazines KNOW that if they are going to survive, they have to get new, younger readers and I'm happy as a salami at a mustard party to help do that for them.

Greenwoman: I got to read your book, Kiss My Aster: A Graphic Guide to Creating a Fantastic Yard Totally Tailored to You, before I sent it to Dan Murphy, who reviews it in this issue. I found it charming, witty, and a great primer for the beginner gardener who wants to dive into creating their own landscape but who needs a helping hand. How did the idea for a book come about?

A.T.: I was dreaming about how to make books more interactive when I thought of the idea. Originally it was going to be SO comprehensive that I thought I'd need help writing it. You know, a backyard bible of sorts. Then I got this wack-a-doo idea of having this hipster gardening book that was illustrated with, you know those terrible IKEA instructions with no words and very vague symbolism? I wanted to do it like that. Carleen Madigan at Storey literally found me in a dumpster and asked me if I had ideas for books, we met up in Boston while I was there speaking and I just LOVED her. She was totally the midwife of this book (to which she would reply that that is disgusting). I literally wrote the whole book for her and if I could make her laugh then I was golden. I wrote the whole book and then they found the illustrators, which completely adds everything. The illustrations are WAY better than the writing!

Greenwoman: What was the most fun part of writing your first book?

A.T.: Hands down, the funniest part was the timing. I had a year to write the book and 10 months to make and give birth to a baby. Simultaneously. I can say, with confidence, that even those closest to me didn't think I could do it. TAKE THAT, HATERS!

Greenwoman: What was the least fun?

A.T.: For the most part, the book was a breeeeeeeeeeeze to write. I just talked out loud to myself about what I'd say to someone asking the questions and wrote it down. People ask, "Oh, isn't it hard to write a book?" Ah, not this one.

But when it came to researching the height and widths of trees and shrubs for the whole country and not just my area? I remember having to dye my hair pink to just have a diversion. It was tedious stuff, and I hate tedious!

Greenwoman: Another thing I am highly impressed with is your treasure trove of kitschy-fab garden imagery (See Kiss My Aster's Facebook photo hoard). You have well over a thousand highly share-able, comment-able visuals from zombie gnomes (also gnome tattoos and murdered gnomes) to vintage garden cheesecake images, and everything in-between. Could you talk a little about your love of imagery and vintage?

AT: I remember the year we got cable TV; I was going into 7th grade. My sister and I were OBSESSED with TCM and watched old movies (with an emphasis on Esther Williams!) all summer instead of playing outside. That was the start of a lot of my hoarding, both images and stuff. I love glamor, I love fun. I love to keep it light. My house is an amazing shrine to me, filled with beautiful vintage tschotske next to a Darth Vader helmet, next to an inflatable Hello Kitty. Plus, I wear vintage just about every day.

Greenwoman: I'm wondering if there's a serious gardener out there who has not seen one of your Ryan Gosling "Hey, Girl" gardening memes. I know I've shared a few! How did that get started?

AT: Oh man! I was at work, driving down Old Elm in Lake Forest, Illinois and the idea just hit me. I pulled over and took notes in my phone. When I got home, I begged Dan to watch Hazel while I made the first crop of them. I posted them and then immediately went on a totally extravagant, totally unlike me and unaffordable, girls' weekend with my bestie in New Orleans. My phone was going bazoinkers the whole time I was there! It was very cool.

I clearly did not drink enough while I was there if I remember all that. A certain unnamed bestie DID drink enough to not remember it, though.

Greenwoman: Finally, what's germinating for you now? Do you have another book in the works?

I'm in love with a new book idea that's in my head right now, I hope they'll let me do it. It's the kind of book I'd shit myself over if I saw it for sale and that's what I aim for! Mainly, I'm taking 2013 to trick out some rad new gardens at my new house.

Greenwoman: I'd love to pry for details on the book idea but I won't—I'll eagerly await the surprise instead! Thanks so much, Amanda, for having a chat with us today! ❀

A few of the many charming looks of Amanda Thomsen.

Buckley's
HOMESTEAD SUPPLY

- Beekeeping supplies
- Soap making supplies
- Cheese and yogurt making supplies
- Organic feed for goats, rabbits and chickens
- Canning and fermenting supplies
- And much, much more!

(719) 358-8510 • 1501 W. Colorado Ave., Colorado Springs, CO
www.buckleyshomesteadsupply.com

The Creature
Feature

Be Careful of Little Lives

by
DB Rudin

Go to the ant, you sluggard; consider her ways and be wise:
Which, having no chief, overseer, or ruler,
Provideth her meat in the summer, [and] gathereth her food in the harvest.
(Proverbs 6:6-6:8)

Scripture praises ants, children are mesmerized by them, and yet ants in the garden are so commonplace as to be easily ignored by us adults. That however, would be a lost opportunity. Ants provide us a chance to witness the spectacle of miniature empires rising and falling in our own backyard.

It is not news that an individual ant is possessed of amazing physical abilities for its size. Scientists have put Weaver Ants upside down on glass where they can not only hold on but support 100 times their own weight. (Their secret is a liquid secreted from their feet.) However, ants don't come into their glory as individuals; they all live in colonies and it is here that they shine.

There are ant colonies numbering only a few hundred individuals that fit into a single acorn (*Temnothorax longispinosus*) and others that include millions of individuals living in vast subterranean cities. One such Grasscutter Ant megalopolis was found abandoned in Argentina. Scientists pumped concrete into the entrances for days and when dry they carefully dug away the surrounding dirt. What they found was astonishing, a vast city where the ants had removed over forty tons of soil. It featured pathways and chambers that stretched down over 25 feet below ground. All accomplished without a central authority directing the activity.

It is easy to get swept away by the shock and awe of statistics, but it is the myriad ways that ants make a living that fascinates me. There are ant societies who make their communal living as farmers, ranchers, hunters and even slave raiders. One stormy July afternoon I discovered the hidden kingdom of the Citronella ants, but that is a story for later.

> Due to their complexity, ant societies are often thought of as the closest to human societies. And, like human societies, they have gone from strict hunters and gatherers to agriculturalists.

Due to their complexity, ant societies are often thought of as the closest to human societies. And, like human societies, they have gone from strict hunters and gatherers to agriculturalists. Some of the most successful ants farm fungus in underground gardens. They feed their fungus grass or leaves harvested from their surroundings. Most amazing is that the fungus exists nowhere else in nature, besides the ants' guts and their fungus gardens, and the ants must fight off other types of fungus and bacteria that threaten these gardens. They do this by applying their own form of antibiotics to any newly added plant material. They also have created ventilation systems that cleverly draw in fresh air and vent out carbon dioxide. This system is so efficient that over five million individuals may occupy a single colony.

There are not only farmers in the ant world, but ranchers as well. Their "livestock" are mealy bugs and aphids. These insects suck the sap from plants and then excrete excess sugar which the ants lap up. The ants in return protect their charges from predators and even hide them under leaves during rain. The ants pick up and move their livestock to "fresh pastures," parts of the plants with more, and/or sweeter, sap. When the ants move they take their livestock with them.

Some ant societies have a more martial flair. They are highly mobile "armies" moving the entire colony on a regular basis, looking for fresh hunting grounds. These "Army Ants" not only feed themselves, hunting anything they can overpower, but many species of birds make a living following the ants around as well. Insects fleeing the ants are then snapped up by the birds. In fact there is a whole family of antbirds, *Thamnophilidae*, with over 200 members. There are antwrens, antshrikes, antvireos and the list goes on. Clearly it is a successful strategy to follow around hunting colonies of army ants.

Pushing the edge of the fantastic is the story of various slave raider ants. These ants raid other ant colonies and steal their eggs and pupae. They return to their own nests and tend the captives. When these captives are born, they are so immersed in the chemical cocktail of their captors' colony that they assume they belong. Some slave raiders have become such specialized warriors that they can no longer take care of themselves. They rely completely on their slaves to gather food and even to feed them. One example from the United States, Polyergus breviceps, won't even clean up after themselves or feed their queen without ant slaves from the genus Formica.

Colorado's "monsoon" season provides the backdrop to a tale of intrigue and power. To tell that tale I must return to the Citronella Ants. Great thunderstorms erupt in July and August dumping torrential rains. Many animals depend upon these rains, including ants. One July afternoon, out hiking in our neighboring Garden of the Gods Park, I came across small, uneven holes in the dirt. Clustered around the entrance were tiny, exquisitely golden ants. I had never seen anything quite like them. Days later I came back and they were gone.

It would be another year before I had the chance to unravel this little local mystery. This time, as thunderheads again threatened, not only did I rediscover the golden ants, but small black winged ants poured out of the misshapen holes. I then started noticing larger, solitary reddish colored ants running around in the same area. One found a hole and, bypassing the golden and winged black ants, disappeared down it. I took pictures and started sending them off to myrmecologists, ant scientists, hoping someone would have a clue as to what was going on.

Turns out these ants are known as Citronella Ants, *Lasius latipes*, (they have an alarm pheromone that smells strongly of citronella). They are completely subterranean except during the monsoon season when the reproductive winged males and larger virgin queens take off for their nuptial flights. The black males die shortly after mating, their role in the story over. The queens' stories, however, are just beginning. After landing they rub off their wings, and unlike other ant queens, they don't build their own nest but rather plot a coup.

This antique illustration is of some honeypot ants.

The ones hanging from the ceiling are known as repletes and they act as living storage containers for nectar or sugar derived from aphids or scale insects.

The queen I observed stealing into the nest was on a mission. Most likely she was from another species of *Lasius* ant. Wafting her own chemical scent, she would seek to woo the small golden female workers while hunting the resident queen. If successful, she would kill the reigning monarch and take over egg laying duties, her off-spring slowly replacing those of the former queen. All the ants will return underground, regardless of the success or failure of the coup attempt, and continue their existence, herding their aphids and scale insects who feed on sap from plant roots. The entire colony and their "livestock" won't visit the light of day again until the monsoons return again next year.

In our gardens, ants are the great equalizers. By hunting insects that become temporarily more populous, they make sure no one group of insects gets out of hand. Their tunnels aerate soil and allow water to penetrate more easily. They have been around for over 100 million years and have formed complex relationships in the environment, many of these we are still discovering. So should you find ants in the garden, relax, they belong there. If you should find them in the house, remember the words of perhaps the most famous ant scientist, Nobel Prize winner E.O. Wilson. When asked what to do if you find ants in your kitchen, Wilson replied "Be careful of little lives." ❀

The first reviews are in!

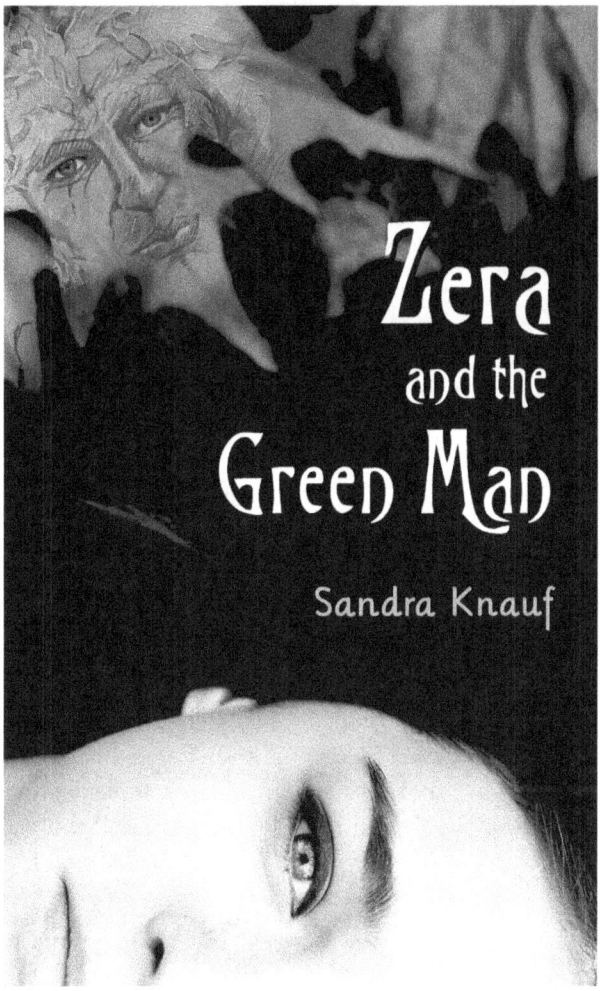

"An ambitious sci-fi novel that will charm eco-champions . . . "
–*Kirkus Reviews*

". . . . will leave readers hoping for a sequel."
–*BlueInk Review*

"The minor characters are exquisite: lively, entertaining, and complex."
–*San Francisco Book Review*

". . . one of those books that you'll want to pass on to your friends."
–Samantha Rivera for *Readers' Favorite* (five star review)

Dearest Mary

by
James A. Ciletti

Dearest Mary,

At 6:30 this morning, I started to write a summer poem for you. I had the very best of intentions and if I were a fine painter I'd have started with our bedroom, morning light through the blinds onto the white sheets covering all of you except one bare leg, beautiful skin, angled out, and your face, haloed with dark hair, so soft in the morning light.

But such a scene eludes my painting skills.

I took my notebook, put a pen in my pocket, and headed for the patio. But passing through the kitchen I stopped to make a pot of coffee. Then, outside I had to drag the sprinkler and hose to the front yard, make sure the chug-chug spitz-spitz spits of spray hit the dry spots, and then I came to the patio to write a poem. I opened my notebook to a page of clean white paper and then inhaled the aroma of coffee.

In the kitchen, I poured my coffee. In my mind's eye I saw you roll so that your face looked up at me and you smiled.

Coffee in hand I returned to the patio.

At the table, notebook before me, pen in hand, I looked out to the garden. I wanted to see the zucchini blossoms we'll make with eggs for breakfast. Of course I had to inspect the green tomatoes. I had to calculate the days and nights until they burst ripe red in your mouth. I will kiss you then.

I walked barefoot in the wet grass. The cool lush green rush of a summery chill tickled my feet, goose-bumped my legs. Is this the same when I kiss your neck?

Finally I was ready to write. But first I had to reposition the spitting sprinkler, and I needed more coffee, that aroma of Jakarta. Out the kitchen window I watched a red-throated finch pecking the first of the dry sunflowers for seeds. I had to wait for him to finish, else opening the screen door might shoo him away.

Out on the patio, the distant drone of a single-engine airplane. Closer, the clash of cars shushing up Union Boulevard set me off, and the shriek of the very close flicker and right beside me the gurgle-urgle of the water fountain girl pouring water, ceaselessly, gurgle gurgle, and closer yet, the silence of my hand's shadow gliding across this page. Yes, Mary, I awoke with the best intentions, to write a poem for you.

By now, both of your bare legs are angled out from the milky sheets. The bees are working in the sunflowers, tomatoes, and zucchini blossoms. The green beans need picked, and I'm about to go inside with an empty coffee cup.

In the bedroom, I will awake you with my kisses.

"On Wings" by Michelle Potter

Greenwoman Magazine

Escape to the garden.

Deputy Editor Zora Knauf, with her sidekick Chancho, at **Greenwoman**'s Vermijo Community Garden plot, September 2012. *Photo by Paul Spielman.*

Organic Lawn & Supply
by Rob Schultz

She peers out of clear
plate-glass, pretty,
hair parting air
of the place, barn-like
old-time general store.

A gentleness here
makes do with well-known
things: hammers like
steel woodpeckers, rakes
shyly fanning themselves,

wrenches long bones
of cattle; a solitary bird-
bath is serene among glaze,
glue, gum, hooks and shackles,
compost and tree-stake kits,

seeds—and plenty of manure.
She turns from the window
and rings up my sale,
smiling, and I feel
red-faced and unsure,

as before anything real.

The Whole Ruth

by Sandra Knauf

Illustration by Laura Chilson

It's 1975 and Ruth Stout, in her early 90s, is being filmed at her home. She's explaining her daily schedule, how many hours a day she works to maintain, harvest, and freeze food from a 45 x 50 foot vegetable garden which grows enough food for two people. (She hasn't been in a grocery store for 14 years.) She also has a few flower beds to take care of, does all her own housework and cooking, and because she's a well-known author, answers a lot of mail.

The show-stopping remark is that she says she never does any of this after 11:00 in the morning:

"Now your hands are going to go up and ask me what time I get up. My answer is to that is sometime between six and eight, according to when I feel like it and when I want to. And the first thing is a long, leisurely breakfast, Roman style, stretched out on the couch; but I'm all through with all of this by 11:00 in the morning. And then she reveals the secret, a secret that has made her a household name:

"The reason [I can do this] is that I never had to plow, or spade, or cultivate, or weed, or hoe, or use fertilizer, or use a poison spray, or use a compost pile, or water. I just plant and pick. The reason that I can do all this is because I keep the ground covered all year long in hay mulch—which rots, fertilizes the ground, keeps down the weeds, keeps the ground soft, and that's all there is to it."

In one paragraph, that's Ruth Stout's famous "no-work" gardening method. Of course, it isn't quite that easy—one would have to buy and bring in hay, and there are other gardening chores (maintaining structures, dealing with wildlife, plucking out the occasional weed, etc.)—but Ruth Stout's "no-work" garden method was very close to that claim.

I first discovered her method in the 1990s, when I became interested in gardening. I didn't have a garden yet, but I was eager to learn. Having no mentors, I trolled the libraries and used bookstores for instruction (this was pre-YouTube times) and found Ruth Stout's books—in abundance. I learned her first book, *How to have a Green Thumb without an Aching Back: A New Method of Mulch Gardening* (first published in 1955 by Exposition Press) was reprinted for decades and sold tens of thousands of copies. She wrote two more books

on gardening, the second expanding on the first, and the third a compilation of articles and essays she'd written over the years for *Organic Gardening and Farming* magazine.

Digging in to Ruth's work, I discovered not only sage instruction, but a kind mentor. She was, like her method, 100% natural, plain-spoken, amusing. She did it, so could you! I was hooked.

Imagine that [1950s] period—Mad Men style mass marketing, food becoming less about nutrition and more about new-fangled products (like Cheez Whiz, Eggo waffles, Mrs. Paul's fish sticks, and TV dinners).

I've in corporated her mulching methods into my gardening ever since.

Ruth Stout's first book came out when she was over sixty years old, during the 1950s, a time when industrial farming and American consumerism was kicking into high gear. Imagine that period—Mad Men style mass marketing, food becoming less about nutrition and more about new-fangled products (like Cheez Whiz, Eggo waffles, Mrs. Paul's fish sticks, and TV dinners). Backyard gardening focused on what new chemical fertilizer, bug killer, or new gas-powered machine could make your tasks easier. You can bet Ruth had her detractors, those who found her simple ways to be too out of touch. America wanted to go forward, not backward.

I wanted to write about the life of my earliest gardening heroine, and so I re-read Stout's gardening books and dove into her writings on other subjects. (She penned a total of nine books over twenty years, all autobiographical, but only three on gardening.)

Ruth Stout was one of the best-known American garden writers in the last century, but, more than that, she was a free-thinking, self-reliant, *original*. For those of us who have been around a few decades, I ask: Can you think of any other woman, born in the Victorian era, who would declare she wasn't into the Women's Movement (of the 1970s) because she felt that "she had been liberated from birth"?

I give you Ruth Stout.

Mama's Girl

Ruth Stout was born in Girard, Kansas on June 14, 1884. She was the fifth of nine children born to Quaker parents John Wallace Stout and Lucetta Elizabeth Todhunter Stout.

> . . . Ruth's mother did not have a problem with other activities that raised eyebrows— such as card-playing, or dancing, or even, at one point, joining Carrie Nation on one of her saloon-smashing, pre-Prohibition raids.

Stout's father was a teacher, then a principal, and for many years the County Superintendent of Schools in their area. Ruth's parents were college educated and the family was middle class, but with so many children, they were not very comfortable financially. John Stout did, however, indulge in a library of 5,000 books, something that all the Stout children would benefit from. Ruth said her mother once commented, "John never has had anything but books or children," which Ruth said was close to the truth.

Ruth was clever and smart, but her older sister May was the leader, her younger sister Juanita got the attention for her beauty, and then there was baby sister Mary. Ruth said she knew from an early age that she would have to distinguish herself in other ways. She enjoyed writing and said that as a high-schooler, she was a "pushover for doing essays for several of her classmates." She tells a story where one girl asked her so often to help her out that she became "fed up, and wrote

one for her about how ignoble, dishonorable (and a few other adjectives) it was to submit a theme you hadn't written yourself." Ruth was sure that would end the problem, but the girl used the essay, thinking it was funny, and even pestered her for more.

Without a doubt, the person who had the biggest influence on Ruth was her mother. Lucetta Stout is mentioned in several of Ruth's books and is the subject of her 1975 biography *As We Remember Mother*. Ruth wrote that her mother was an "indifferent housekeeper and cook" (a trait Ruth admitted sharing, along with her mother's vegetarianism) who never scolded her children but knew how to use reason and gentleness to make them behave. Lucetta Stout was deeply religious, non-judgmental of others, and vehemently anti-war. She did not attend church often and never pushed her beliefs on others. Ruth said she simply adhered to the Quaker belief that people would do well if they followed their "inner voice" (conscience). This "voice," the Quakers believed, changed and grew as individuals headed (hopefully) towards "fuller understanding" in their life's journey.

Ruth's mother nurtured the creative spark in all of her children, encouraging them, for example, when they became obsessed with theater, to recreate skits they had seen, and even write and produce their own. The children's plays became so popular that when they lived in Topeka they would put on several performances of each production, seating 50 people at a time. Many in the family would remain interested and active in entertainment in adulthood, and the family continued putting on their own productions for their own amusement, for decades. This environment spurred several of them to write professionally, and Ruth's younger brother Rex Stout became a famous mystery writer (he authored the Nero Wolfe mysteries from 1934 to 1975).

While the family grew up in the infamously rigid Victorian era, Ruth's mother did not have a problem with other activities that raised eyebrows—such as card-playing, dancing, or even, for a brief period, joining Carrie Nation on one of her saloon-smashing, pre-Prohibition raids. Wrote Ruth, "One had to know Mother rather well to realize that she followed nobody's rules, not even God's, without giving them some thought—to find out if they made sense to her."

On the Way to NYC

After graduating high school, Ruth considered joining a traveling vaudeville group whose show included a fake mind-reading act. While other family members were alarmed (especially since the man who wanted Ruth as an assistant seemed to have dishonorable designs) her parents did not intervene. When a friend of Lucetta Stout's confronted her, Mrs. Stout said if she couldn't trust her own children then who would? She also reportedly laughed, and added: "Anyway, you don't need to worry about Ruth; she isn't going to let a man even kiss her until she's safely married to him."

Ruth heard this and said her "mouth dropped open in amazement." It was true, she had never even kissed a boy, but she was shocked that her mother knew about that particular pledge she had made to herself.

Ruth didn't join the act, but decided to head to New York soon after when her brother Rob and his wife Esther came through town. The couple had worked their way to Topeka reading palms (which Ruth acknowledged was a scam that everyone in their family was aware of, including her mother, who, again, "didn't say a word").

The trio ran out of money in Kansas City and Ruth found work as a nursemaid. There she received her first lesson on America's class system. The first day at work she got the baby to bed and asked if she could help the cook. The cook asked her to set the table but Ruth made a huge mistake that stunned the lady of the house—she set a place for herself and the cook at the family table. Ruth wrote that another time she was running a bath for herself and her mistress knocked on the door, telling her she must not use the bathtub. Ruth apologized and asked where to find her bathtub. "That threw her, since I didn't have one, and after clearing her throat a few times she said I could use that one, if I left it very clean."

Before too long the group left Kansas City. Around Christmastime they got to Indianapolis. Here again, they ran into a money-snag when they discovered it wasn't easy to sell fortune-telling during the holiday season (amazingly, people were more concerned about buying presents). Ruth found work in a department store, and after the Christmas season, a position at the phone company. Not long after that, her father, who had quit his school work and became a traveling salesman, and her mother, her brother Donald, and little sister Mary came to live in Indianapolis as well. Ruth notes in a book written later in her life that her scam-artist brother, who was constantly pawning his wife's engagement ring during the journey, turned out to be in later years a "wealthy, upstanding citizen."

The pilgrimage to New York City would be delayed in Indianapolis for the next five years. In 1909, the oldest child of the Stout family died. May was eight years older than Ruth and Ruth considered her a "second mother." "One day we got a telegram saying May had died in her sleep. I have never loved anyone else quite the way I cared for her, and that's all I want to say about that." In another book Ruth confesses that she was devastated by not only loss, but guilt. May, who had recently visited Indiana, had asked Ruth to help her get a job at the phone company so she could move to Indianapolis too. Although she had recently started practicing medicine in Colorado, she was having trouble with the doctor she was working with and knew the partnership

> The trio ran out of money in Kansas City and Ruth found work as a nursemaid. There she received her first lesson on America's class system.

would soon be dissolved. Ruth, making the judgment that her gifted sister needed to stay in medicine, and not wanting her to move in with them, refused to help. Hence, Ruth blamed herself, until her mother spoke to her about it. Lucetta Stout told her daughter that even if a person didn't believe in immortality surely they believed that good memories kept a loved one alive in their minds and hearts. She said that it would be a shame if the many good memories of May were overshadowed by this misunderstanding. Ruth wrote, "That straightened me out."

New York City

Soon after May's death, the family made the move to New York City. Their new home would be a four-story brownstone on West 118th St., less than a block from Morningside Park (designed by the famous American landscaper Frederick Law Olmsted). Ruth would live in New York City for the next twenty years.

That first year, before they were settled in socially, the family amused themselves at Sunday dinner by taking turns giving spontaneous speeches, or by reading aloud something they had written on a chosen topic. Some of these poems and essays were so entertaining they found publication in the local paper.

Ruth and her mother also attended spiritualist meetings. These were gatherings which operated around the belief that the dead could communicate with the living— i. e., séances—and were very popular from the 1840s through the 1920s with middle and upper class women, many who were supporters of women's suffrage movement, and, earlier, the abolitionist movement. "Mother and I both became fascinated with spiritualist meetings," wrote Stout. " . . . in NYC in the days before TV and radio you either went to church or a spiritualist meeting if you were a stranger in town and not established yet."

Ruth's mother liked to keep an open mind about everything, proven or not, and during the New York years explored the subjects of psychoanalysis, hypnotism,

like to bet that those who do get something real and lasting out of their studies would have got something just as worthwhile out of those four years if they had spent them another way. . ."

Indeed, all the Stout children seemed to have enjoyed interesting, productive lives and several achieved fame and/or financial success. Ruth's brother Rex, the mystery writer (who was also a child prodigy in mathematics) and his brother Robert devised a school banking system in the early 1900s. It was a cooperative program between banks and schools that encouraged children to save and it made them enough money for Rex to move to Paris and write full-time. A few years down the road, Robert became a banker.

Ruth spent most of the New York years working in various offices and writing occasionally for publication. By the time she was in her late thirties she was

"What is so wonderful about youth? Little chickens are cute, but they can't lay eggs; kittens are adorable but they're not wise like cats . . . flowers have to mature before they give you blossoms."

chiropractic (which was then new), magnetic healing, and more. She never, as Ruth puts it, "went overboard" for any of these subjects, but had the philosophy that there was something good in everything and all study and experiences brought a wider understanding of life.

The family bought a player-piano, for their sparsely-furnished though spacious home, on the installment plan. One of the rooms on the 2nd floor was "immense" and so they installed the piano there and dubbed it "the ballroom." Another second-story room was called the library. Ruth remembers those years of being full of young visitors, including brothers and sisters and their children, with lots of dances and parties.

Everyone at the townhouse had jobs except Donald, who was in high school. Donald would later be allowed to drop out of school to pursue his love, which was zoology. Ruth, who never went to college, later wrote: "Mother and Dad had both gone to college but their children had not been willing to waste time sitting around in a college classroom when Life was right there on the doorstep challenging us to come on out and see what we could do with it." Later she would give a less boisterous opinion: "I believe that many young people graduate without having been changed in any way that is going to make a particle of difference in their lives. And I would

making a living, "of sorts," writing short stories and decided to start her own business, a tearoom. She and a friend opened the "Will 'O the Wisp," but soon found out it didn't provide an income for two people. Ruth ventured out on her own, opening a tea room she named the Klicket. She described the venture as taking all of her capital, about the equivalent of $1,000 today. The tearoom was located in a "gloomy" and "dilapidated" Greenwich Village building, but Ruth said it "reeked with atmosphere." Neighborhood tearooms were popular gathering places for artists and other interesting people after WWI, and Ruth made a lot of friends.

Perhaps Ruth's greatest hardship during the New York years was losing her brother Donald, the youngest of the Stout children, to tuberculosis. He died when he was only 19 years old. Ruth said her mother handled this well, telling the distraught doctor who had cared for him, "I haven't lost him."

Later she would share that she had a harder time in her 20s than any time in her life—more times of despair and even thoughts of suicide. Once she remarked on youth in general: "What is so wonderful about youth? Little chickens are cute, but they can't lay eggs; kittens are adorable but they're not wise like cats . . . flowers have to mature before they give you blossoms."

Rebel, Rebel

Ruth's New York City occupations included bookkeeper at a department store, secretary, business manager, and factory worker. She confessed that she bluffed her way into the bookkeeping job after her brother Rex told her she should apply because it paid better than work for "office girls." He offered to help her out if she got "stumped." Ruth was able to fake it until she made it, eventually being promoted to head of that department, and in charge of eleven "girls." (Women workers at that time were commonly referred to as "girls.")

Business was booming and they all worked very hard, especially in the busy season, putting in overtime hours for no additional pay.

Ruth Stout (from a family portrait), circa 1905.

Because of this, Ruth thought it would be fair to allow the women to run the occasional personal errand during slow periods. Ruth almost lost her job over this until she asked her supervisor if he would prefer that they stick to regular hours (8:30 A. M. to 6 P. M. year-round—regular hours were also longer in pre-union America) and not have the work finished during the busy season, and have the workers sit idle when work was light. She won her argument, and got to do things her way. After that, the office manager made a habit of coming in and standing and glaring at the women (which made them all nervous) until Ruth began asking about raises when he visited. Ruth described her office as an "independent kingdom" where they "got the work done on time, and correctly, but beyond that, we did exactly as we pleased." This lasted for seven years.

Ruth wrote: "It wasn't surprising that he, and the other bosses, didn't interfere with us; they obviously sensed something that was a settled fact, although my staff and I never discussed it. It was just this: we stood together and we knew our power. What did surprise me was that although all of the other departments in the store were very envious of us, none of them made any attempt to emulate us."

She said that this experience, among others, taught her that it was a mistake to submit to things you do not agree with (unless you had no choice), and more importantly, it taught her the importance of thinking for oneself.

At a subsequent job, Ruth claimed she had a college degree so she could apply to head an office of twenty girls selling advertisements for a newspaper. She justified her lie, writing that she knew what the employer really wanted was to make sure that the applicants were literate, which she certainly was, even more so than many college graduates. The work load was "incredibly light," so she began to write at her desk for other publications. This lasted until she was discovered and fired. Later she wrote a story about that experience, and one magazine she submitted it to rejected it on the basis that it was "too farfetched."

Her autobiography mentions eccentricities, such as eating only raw foods for a while (to save time), and working in a monotonous and underpaid factory job for a year because she felt everyone should experience factory work if they used factory-made products. That year, in which she was "bored to tears on a daily basis," Ruth's job was to refill a pot of glue (the company made envelopes). She said for the rest of her life she had an aversion to using envelopes, preferring postcards for correspondence.

The Love of her Life

From the written evidence (her own accounts), it seems that it was only when Ruth was in her late 30s that her teenage pledge to not kiss a man until she was married was put to the test. While she did have suitors, all were far from the "prince" she'd been waiting for. And when she did meet her prince, he came with a problem.

Ruth met Alfred (Fred) Rossiter, when he first visited her tearoom with his wife. Fred claimed it was love at first sight for him and began visiting regularly. It wasn't long before Ruth discovered she felt the same. Ruth wrote that Fred had been in an unhappy marriage for a long time and when he met Ruth he asked his wife for a divorce; ". . . [Fred's wife] refused, and included some fainting spells and so on, and he and I saw each other a few times and then had a sad parting." Ruth was heartbroken. The two did not see each other, or even correspond, for seven long years.

Only one year after they parted, in 1923, the still-lovesick Ruth was talking to her mother about her fondness of Dostoevsky and the Russian novelists, and her mother suggested she visit Russia. The Quakers were there, doing famine-relief work, and Mrs. Stout felt sure that Ruth could go there as a volunteer. Ruth jumped at the suggestion and within a month she was on her way. She found she loved the Russian people, whom she described as kind, helpful, and not "as restricted by rules of behavior as Americans are." The poverty she witnessed, however, shocked her. Ruth worked at the Grachovka children's home, which cared for about 200 orphans. All of the children had lost their parents to starvation (in most instances, the parents had sacrificed food to keep their children alive) and, as Ruth put it, were now being fed by the Quakers. What struck Ruth (at 91 she said she still felt emotional about it) was that these children, having no other pictures, would take the labels from American food cans to embellish their walls. Not because they were hungry, but because they had nothing else decorative.

This visit was one of the transformative events in Ruth Stout's life. She would always have a special fondness for the Russian people and had little tolerance for those who criticized them during the Cold War. When the topic came up, Ruth would ask if the person had ever actually visited Russia. Without fail, they would say no. "My advice to anyone who is criticizing Russia," she wrote, "would be don't spend your time worrying about your neighbor's dirty house; get out the broom and clean your own."

When she returned from Russia, her brother Rex thought he could distract her from thoughts of Fred Rossiter (who was still very much under her skin) by getting her interested in the Socialist movement, then enjoying great popularity in the United States. (As an aside, Rex Stout's own left-wing interests, which included leadership in the Authors League of America, would earn him a file in J. Edgar Hoover's collection from the 1930s on.) This scheme worked well, and Ruth spent a couple of weeks at a summer camp that year for socialist and trade union activists put on by the Rand School.

At the camp, Ruth fell under the spell of the well-known Socialist speaker Scott Nearing, who lectured on Russia. The two connected over Russia, their shared vegetarianism, and became smitten with each other. Unfortunately, Nearing, like Rossiter, was married. Ruth writes in her last book, published when she was 91, and 15 years after her husband's death, that they shared some kisses, but nothing else.

During the camp visit, Ruth saw that the people running the socialist camp were hypocritical regarding class-consciousness. For example, they had a creed—"For each, according to his ability, to each according to his needs," yet she observed that the elevator man (who had three kids and a sick wife) still received far less pay than the manager. Furthermore, when they had group

> "My advice to anyone who is criticizing Russia," she wrote, "would be don't spend your time worrying about your neighbor's dirty house; get out the broom and clean your own."

meals, the "help" was served a different meal than the rest. She was disappointed in the movement, calling herself, at her age, too optimistic and naïve. "I thought I had finally found a group of people who actually followed their own rules."

During this stage in her life, she also realized she liked "hours better than dollars," so got a half-time job, lived frugally, and discovered she was free to do what she pleased the rest of the day. What she pleased to do turned out to be working for Nearing and the Socialist magazine *The New Masses* as a full-time, unpaid secretary. Although she had feelings for Nearing, Ruth wrote that romance was not her motivation. She said, Nearing was "a great pleasure but the most interesting part of all was his lectures and debates."

Ruth had the same insight with "liberals" as she did with Socialists. She once went to The Liberal Club in NYC, observed a lot of name-dropping, and thought to herself, "They are no different from the common herd

. . . My guess was that they scorned people who had to keep up with the Joneses, by buying a certain make of car and so on and on, but they were doing exactly the same thing—showing off their close relationship with the 'right' kind of human beings. I suppose I should

> ## . . . when Fred told Ruth about Emily Post, the leading authority on socially correct etiquette in America, Ruth was flabbergasted that people actually read books telling them how to behave.

have known that but I had overlooked it."

Seven years after they parted, Ruth contacted Fred by letter (she asserts in her autobiography that she had no ulterior motive, but only wanted to see how he was doing) to learn he had left his wife. The two met, discovered that they were still in love, and got back together. It would take another three years and much difficulty before Fred was granted a divorce.

Ruth wrote that she stayed at Fred's apartment most of the time after they got back together, even though she "officially" lived at home. Her parents knew about the arrangement (which could not have been easy in the 1920s), but her mother never spoke about it. One day Ruth could take it no longer. She confronted her mother, saying, "I'm afraid you're concerned about Fred and me, Mother, but isn't it true that, through your life, if you were doing something which you believed was all right, you would keep on, even if the whole world thought you were wrong? Well, it's your hard luck that you have a daughter exactly like you in that one respect."

After that, Mr. and Mrs. Stout visited the couple at Fred's apartment. In fact, Fred and Lucetta Stout became great friends.

Ruth and Fred married in June, 1929. Ruth was 45 years old.

Country Life with Fred

The Stock Market Crash of 1929 hit everyone hard, including the newlyweds. In early 1930, they moved to the outskirts of Redding, Connecticut, to a 55-acre farm for their retirement. They, like many during that time, felt they could live cheaply off the land.

That spring, Ruth planted her first garden and she and Fred adjusted to married life. Ruth had lived an unfettered life for decades and now had to get used to another's routine and preferences; On the other hand, Fred had married someone who admitted she had little skill or interest in the domestic arts and who was also happily oblivious to the many "rules" of society. As an example, when Fred told Ruth about Emily Post, the leading authority on socially correct etiquette in America, Ruth was flabbergasted that people actually read books telling them how to behave. Fortunately, Ruth's "eccentricities" were ones Fred found charming.

The couple was very social, and for many years they invited all of their friends to join them out in the country whenever they pleased. They renovated a huge barn, installing no-frills bedrooms, a kitchen, and a bathroom. (Later, a painter would turn the barn's loft into a studio, and, for a while, a writer worked in a shack he built himself in the woods on the property.) Ruth said the visitors changed constantly and included artists, writers, a sculptor, dancers, and a slew of what their neighbors referred to as "Foreigners." The visitors came non-stop during the summers, and there was always a "deluge" during the weekends.

The couple didn't ask guests to pitch in for upkeep. Ruth wrote that she and Fred discussed it and worried that if they did, visitors would make demands. This arrangement worked fine, for a while. After some years, it began to get frustrating, especially when things were broken and no one offered to help replace them. (Ruth dryly noted that one man did take it upon himself to screen in the barn's porch, so they wouldn't have to sit out there all the time "slapping mosquitoes.") Needless to say, they were pleased when on the spring of the 8th year, someone put a bank in the barn's kitchen with a note asking for donations. Ruth wrote that she figured if every guest put in a dime for every night they stayed they would receive about 90 dollars by the end of the summer. By the end of the summer they received exactly one dollar and fifty-five cents. "Our first feeling when we opened the bank was astonishment, then some indignation, and finally tolerance," wrote Ruth.

Postcard, circa 1910.

Ruth reveals more about those years in her second book, *Company Coming—Six Decades of Hospitality*, which also covers her mother's experiences as a hostess. Open and honest, Ruth probably made a few former guests squirm when the book came out, but wrote that

Ruth and Fred on the farm.

what she ultimately derived from those years was sharing their lives with others was a highly enriching experience.

Ruth didn't shy away from giving her opinion of the over-privileged, either. She and her husband held several charity events at their farm, until she said they had so many frustrating experiences with the millionaires who were "helping" arrange things, that they quit doing them. In several of her books she disparaged the lack of the practical abilities of those born into privilege. "For help in any situation which takes something more than an adequate bank account to solve, don't give me a person who has never been *obliged* to earn his bread and butter, his place in the world." [Italics are Stout's.] Elsewhere, she wrote, "People brought up with money are completely blind to the biggest problem the majority of humans face, which is the job of somehow getting enough to eat in order to stay alive, and of getting a stove to cook it on, and a chair to sit on while they eat it and a bed to rest on so that they can conserve their energy and be able to join the daily struggle for bread again tomorrow."

In one of her books, Ruth shared some information on her husband's past, namely that he had come from a wealthy family and was reared by a "narrow-minded" English governess. (His mother claimed that she knew nothing about bringing up a son, so didn't.) Fred described his father as good-hearted but lacking in intelligence, and said that snobbishness flourished in the family. Ruth deduced that was why her husband took an opposite path as an adult. "All he needed, in later years, was to come in contact with a laborer who had never read a book to try to make a pal out of him," she wrote, "or at least to have him to dinner, and try to get acquainted with him." Aside from entertaining visitors and doing upkeep on the farm, Fred spent his retirement years following his passion for woodworking. He had a studio in another barn on the property and his wood bowls and other creations received some national recognition.

> "For help in any situation which takes something more than an adequate bank account to solve, don't give me a person who has never been obliged to earn his bread and butter, his place in the world."

After Ruth's father passed away, her mother came to live with them in a separate cottage, along with Mary, Ruth's youngest sister. Lucetta Stout was by all accounts very happy there until World War II began. As someone who hated war, as Ruth put it, in her "heart, mind, bones, and in her very soul," another world conflict proved too much to bear. Almost overnight her mother began to show she wasn't really interested in staying in a world rife with senseless violence. Lucetta Stout drew the curtains at her cottage, ate only under protest, and stopped tending to her flower garden. She died five months later, and the family, especially Ruth and Fred, took it very hard.

Ruth's Big Gardening Break-Through

It was during WWII that Ruth started on a path that would ultimately and completely change her view of how to garden. She said this new vision came about from her own impatience. Every spring she would be eager to plant her vegetable garden, and every spring she first had to wait for the plowman to turn over the earth, as that is how it was done. The growing season was short in Connecticut, and with plowing delayed, it was slightly maddening. In addition, while she was in great health, she was now older (in 1944 she'd turn 60), and she said her huge garden, grown coventionally, was beginning to seem like too much work.

She relates that on that early April day, in the spring of 1944, after 14 years of gardening, she went outside to the garden "to shed a tear" because she couldn't plant yet. While there, she asked the asaparagus, "We don't have to plow for you, why do we have to plow for the other vegetables?" She said the asparagus replied, saying, "You don't. Go ahead and plant." She decided to plant her vegetable seeds then, with no plowing, and waited to see what would happen. Ruth would discover that with her method, annual vegetables and flowers could thrive without plowing. All they needed was straw mulch.

Her first experience was successful enough to encourage her to do more, but it would take a few years to develop and refine her "no-work" method.

A Garden Writer is Born

Excited about her findings, Ruth decided to write a book. She sent a proposal to an editor at Scribner, but he turned her down, saying that they liked the idea but had a professor who was writing a book about mulch.

Ruth thought it highly unlikely that their books were similar, and soon found that to be true—the book by Dr. Pratt of Cornell was not about no-work gardening. She decided she would strike out on her own. Now in her mid-sixties, she self-published her very first book. Later she wrote that she didn't know how she got the money, but that "Fred didn't give it to me because he thought I was crazy."

Fred was mistaken. His wife's self-published book proved successful enough that in 1955 Exposition Press in New York re-published Ruth's book as *How to have a Green Thumb without an Aching Back: A New Method of Mulch Gardening*. Ruth said she thought the title was rather silly, but went along with it. She also kept her maiden name as author, although she was known as Mrs. Rossiter to her neighbors.

She wrote about her first book: "Not only did it sell several hundred thousand copies in hardcover, but is now also in paperback, selling many thousands more. And whenever I go on the air and talk about my way of gardening the station is flooded with letters . . . not that the book is outstanding, but that just people are happy to be told how to accomplish something they want to do but haven't the time for." For many years she said she received hundreds of letters a year, and the ones she liked best were from those from people with a full-time job, a medical condition, or small children, who testified that her method made it possible to garden when otherwise it would have been impossible.

A few years after the first book came out another New York publisher persuaded Ruth to write a second one. Ruth said her sister Mary (who lived in their cottage) made the remark that the whole method had been fully explained in about fifteen hundred words—in

Ruth and her thriving onions.

the first book. Ruth agreed. The publisher insisted that surely Ruth had learned a lot since then. After some reflection, Ruth decided yes, she had more to share.

Lost in the Moment by Leslie Macon

Ruth once heard from a woman who, after learning of her method, wondered about simply tossing some potatoes out in the several-feet-high tall grass meadow near her house and throwing hay on top of them. Ruth said she'd never tried it, so she didn't know whether it would work or not. The woman tried it and wrote, "I had never had such fine potatoes in my life. Nor so many." On this matter, an acquaintance of Ruth's remarked, "Do you know something? At least nine out of ten people would have told her, yes, that was wrong, if they hadn't tried it themselves. You don't make conclusions about anything you don't know about from personal experience."

> "Not only did it sell several hundred thousand copies in hardcover, but is now also in paperback, selling many thousands more . . . not that the book is outstanding, but that just people are happy to be told how to accomplish something they want to do but haven't the time for."

Ruth replied: "Well, I try not to, for I am always 'putting down' the so-called authorities who do just that. . . And because I'm so against people giving advice about things they don't know about personally I'm very glad that I waited several years before I wrote about year-round gardening . . ."

Another insight she had was that by using hay for mulch, which would eventually break down and feed the soil, you were going one-better than those who bought manure for the garden—what's left after the nutrients of the hay are processed by the animal.

Her common-sense, try-it-out-and-see-for-yourself approach also spawned a long-running series of articles in Organic Gardening and Farming magazine (1953-1971). These would later be made into her third and last book on gardening, *The Ruth Stout No-Work Garden Book* (co-authored with Richard Clemence).

Life Without Fred

Fred died on Thanksgiving Day, 1960, after an extended illness. Ruth wrote that he spent five months with an oxygen tent, under the care of the most "inefficient nurse in the world . . . Me." She wrote that he wanted "desperately to die and would have handled that but now that he had gone overboard for Yoga he thought it was wrong to kill himself."

Ruth wrote in her second-to-last book, *I've Always Done It My Way*, that she believed only in two kinds of killing—taking someone's life in self-defense, and mercy-killing (not only for dogs and cats, but for people). She added that she believed that a person should be able to choose suicide.

The year of her husband's death marked the publication of her third book, *It's a Woman's World*, by Doubleday & Co., Inc. Five more books would follow, with Ruth publishing three in her tenth decade.

Though now in her mid-70s, Ruth was fit and had many years ahead of her. A decade later she would relate the story of a doctor telling her after an examination (at age 84), "Well, you're a good healthy 48-year-old."

In one of her books she listed the four things she attributed to good health: good genes, good food, exercise (though she said she never over-did it and found walks boring) and, last, but not least, keeping a positive mental attitude. She said that we couldn't do anything about our inheritance, but we could do something about the other three, especially food. Although she believed in thrift, she special-ordered some food by mail and wrote that ". . . a person who doesn't fool around keeping up with the style and the Joneses can afford to be a spendthrift when it comes to being in good shape. Besides, food is cheaper than a doctor and more enjoyable."

She wrote that she was lucky because keeping a positive mental attitude was easy for her. "I just am, by nature, an optimist. The pleasant idea comes instead of the depressing one." Nevertheless, those later years were a time of loneliness. Ruth wrote that she was glad she had her gardening, writing, and lectures or she wouldn't have had anything to live for after Fred died. She found it vital to be useful and contributing in the world.

Over the years she had more than 7,000 people visit her garden, coming from every state in the U. S. and Canada. She admitted to sometimes being inconvenienced by unannounced guests, but added that she was always happy to see them.

She would continue on at Poverty Hollow with her sister Mary. Mary died in 1977 at age 88 (living at Poverty Hollow for 40 years). Ruth followed her three years later, leaving this world in 1980 at the age of 96.

A Last Word on the Lovely, Naked Ruth

Ruth's belief in doing exactly as she pleased was exhibited in the way she lived her life, and it was certainly the force that enabled her to envision a "no work garden" and to bring that vision into best-selling book form. But there was one more area in which Ruth did as she liked,

didn't come up until six because up until six they were still stopped.' "

In Ruth Stout I found not only a gardening mentor but a mentor on living. In a difficult century for women, she followed her bliss, doing the best she could with what she had, and having a little fun in the process. It made sense to me that it took someone unencumbered with "rules" to see things differently, to create a small no-work gardening revolution all on her own.

A revolution that perfectly reflected her grand philosophy: "If you live your life to suit yourself, how can you possibly fail to make the most of it?" ❁

> "I would go down there to garden and the minute I got down there I would take off all my clothes and garden naked. I've always loved the air on my body. . ."

and this little biography wouldn't be complete without mentioning it—her nude gardening.

She wrote about it in one of her books, but that day in the garden, in her tenth decade, she told about it on camera in Arthur Mokin's award-winning film, *Ruth Stout's Garden*:

"I loved my husband very, very much. I really mean it when I say that I'm sure that he is the only man in the world who could have stood staying married to me because I always was always out of order—I mean the things I did!

"I would go down there to garden and the minute I got down there I would take off all my clothes and garden naked. I've always loved the air on my body. And I never said a word to Fred about it one way or another, it never occurred to me to mention it to him. And I came back every evening around 5:00 o'clock and put my clothes on before I came back. And I one day I came back at six and Fred was out in the barn doing his stuff (he made all these wooden things and so on) and shortly after I got in, he came in and he said, 'Well, you worked longer today, didn't you?'

"And I said, 'But how did you know?' (I was just curious, how did he happen to know.)

"He said, 'It was easy. As a rule, as the cars go along the road after 5:00 they just go on, but up until five o'clock they kind of go very slowly and look down at your garden area. [She laughs heartily.] So I knew you

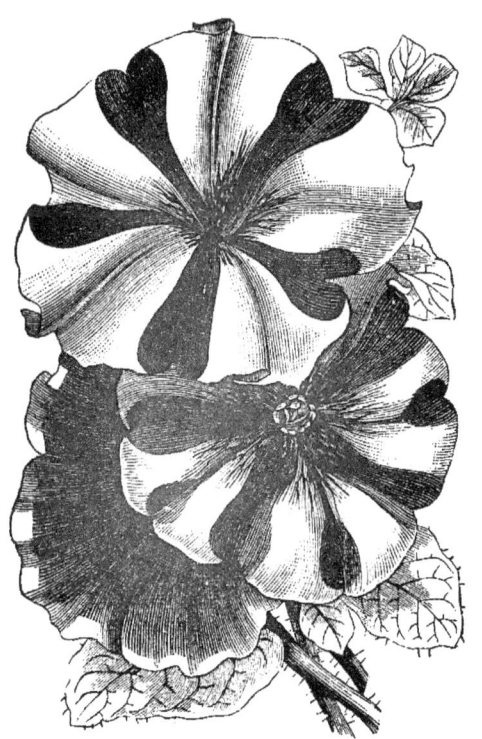

MOM'S FLOCK
Renegade Hens in Highland Park

Mom wasn't dead, but she didn't get out of bed. She refused food, ignored conversation, but aside from Alzheimer's, there was nothing wrong.

Look, Mom. I brought you BABY BIRDS!

Both female. They're baby chickens. When they grow up they'll give us eggs!

Are they male or female?

The BOY is trying to get AWAY. The girl is falling asleep, but HE keeps waking her up.

But can she KEEP them?

NIGHT-TIME CARE-GIVER, CHRIS.

In Warsaw, my chicken and I shared a single potato.

If we have chickens we will not watch so much Dr. Phil.

DAYTIME CAREGIVER, Sunny

U. S. History: Granada Relocation Center, Amache, Colorado.
Mrs. M. Yoshinaga, wife of the unit supervisor, volunteered to weed lettuce.
Department of the Interior. War Relocation Authority. 4 June 1943. Wikimedia Commons.

Anole on a Hydrangea by Leslie Macon

Apples are Ruling My Life

by Pat Cook Gulya

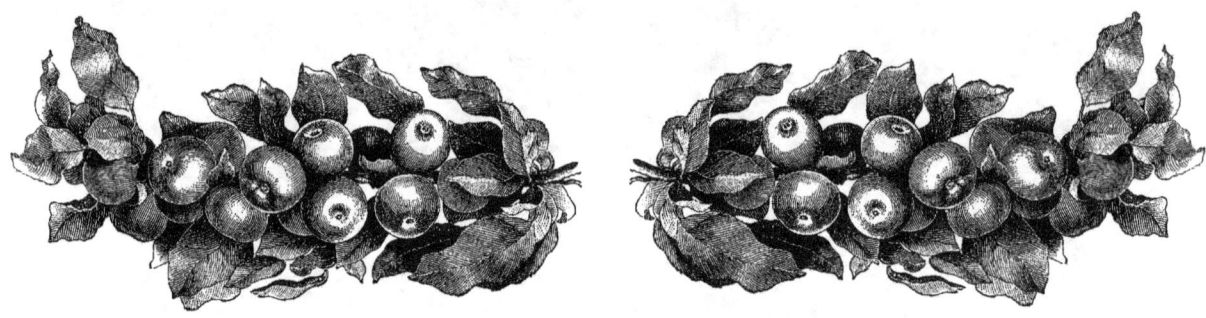

When I close my eyes, I see apples. When I step out my back door, I smell apples. When I look out my front door and windows, I see apples clinging to the trees and lying on the ground. For several weeks as I lie in bed at night I hear them falling, landing with a hollow thud.

We recently moved to five acres in Penrose, Colorado. The half-acre, wedge-shaped orchard has thirty mature trees, twenty-five of them are apple and twenty of those are loaded with fruit.

Everyone I talk to, I ask if they'd like some apples. I cut and core apples for sauce, crisp and pies. I freeze apples; I juice apples, but mostly I pick up and sort apples.

Initially I had three grades; human consumption, horse or deer consumption, and compost. Now that the neighbors' horses are "appled out" and we aren't going to Cedar Heights to feed the deer, I only have two grades; consumption and compost. Wormholes, bird pecks, squirrel bites, bad bruises or sunburn doom an apple to compost.

If I pick up the apples that fall daily, it takes two hours; if I miss a day, it takes four hours. I can empathize with migrant workers and they do this all day every day, with no end in sight. My livelihood doesn't depend on my speed, however my sanity, does, so I try to work as quickly as possible.

The apples are various sizes. I can barely pick up two of the largest ones in one hand, but I can handle six of the smallest. The taste varies too, sweet to puckery. Some have thin skins and other thick, some have small dark hard seeds and others pale soft ones. The colors vary greatly; deep crimson, wine purple, rose to pale green, and light yellow.

As I'm picking up apples, I am sampling the fruits from the trees, determining my favorites. One tree seems to have two different types of apples; on one side, the apples are considerably smaller. Maybe it is the amount of sunlight since I don't see a graft line on the trunk where the branches connect.

One tree is the favorite of the birds. I don't know if that's because of its placement in the orchard (it is shaded by a large elm) or the quality of the apples. There are no apples left on that tree. I didn't like those apples too much; I thought they were mushy.

I had to get a handle on all these apples. The boxes were filling up the garage and I'd contacted everyone I could think of that might like apples. I called Care and Share to see if they were interested in apple donations. The guy I talked to was thrilled. "We'll take all you can bring us," he said. I felt such relief. I'm composting apples that I'd be using in a lean year and feeling guilty about it, so now I can feel good about my apple picking efforts. So far, we've taken three loads of apples to C&S—about 1,000 lbs.

A few weeks ago when one neighbor told me that I should spray my apple trees, I never dreamed that I'd have this many. Of course, I told him no. I want my apples to be organic and safe. It's nice to have plenty to share with the birds, squirrels, rabbits, and, of course, with the hungry people of Colorado Springs.

I figure that I still have a few more weeks of apple-ing before all the trees are bare. The strange thing is that I still love apples. I eat stewed apples everyday for breakfast and have several while I'm working in the orchard. When I get thirsty and come into the house for something to drink, you guessed it—I have apple juice.

I'll enjoy the fruits of this summer all winter and to encourage next year's crop perhaps I'll follow the tradition that Thoreau writes of in his essay, "Wild Apples."

"…on Christmas eve…they salute the apple-trees with much ceremony, in order to make them bear well the next season." This salutation consists in "throwing …cider about the roots of the tree . . . and then, "encircling one of the best bearing trees in the orchard, they drink the following toast several times: —

'Here's to thee, old apple-tree,
Whence thou mayst bud, and whence thou mayst, blow,
And whence thou mayst bear apples enow!
Hats-full! caps-full!
Bushel, bushel, sacks-full!
And my pockets full, too! Hurra!' " ✿

From the Library of Virginia's 1939 *World's Fair Photograph Collection*.
"Eleven million apple trees in virginia produce fine fruit for the markets of the world, with plenty of culls for canneries."

Pleasures of the Nose

by

Louise Beebe Wilder

A garden full of sweet odours is a garden full of charm, a most precious kind of charm not to be implanted by mere skill in horticulture or power of purse, and which is beyond explaining. It is born of sensitive and very personal preferences yet its appeal is almost universal. Fragrtance speaks to many to whom color and form say little, and it "can bring as irresistibly as music emotions of all sorts to the mind." Besides the plants visible to the eye there will be in such a garden other comely growths, plain to that "other sense," such as "faith, romance, the lore of old unhurried times." These are infinitely well worth cultivating among the rest. They are an added joy in happy times and gently remedial when life seems warped and tired.

Nor is the fragrant garden ever wholly our own. It is, whether we will or no, common property. Over hedge or wall, and often far down the highway, it sends a greeting, not alone to us who have toiled for it, but to the passing stranger, the blind beggar, the child skipping to school, the tired woman on her way to work, the rich man, the careless youth. And who shall say that the gentle sweet airs for a moment enveloping them do not send each on his way touched in some manner, cheered, softened, filled with hope or renewed in vigor, arrested perhaps, in some devious course?

In mediaeval times there was a widespread belief in the efficacy of flower and leaf scents as cures or alleviations for all sorts of ills of the flesh, but more especially of the spirit, and as a protection against infection. This belief is testified to again and again in early horticultural and medical works. "If odours may worke satisfaction," wrote Gerard, "they are so sovereign in plants and so comfortable that no confection of apothecaries can equall their excellent virtue." In the *Grete Herball* it is written, "Against weyknesse of the brayne smel to Musk." The scent of Basil was thought stimulating to the heart and "it taketh away melancholy and maketh a man merry and glad." The fragrance of Sweet Marjoram was deemed remedial for those "given to over much sighing." The scent of violets was thought an aid to digestion, and of Rosemary it was written, "Smell of it and it shall keep thee youngly." "As for the garden of Mint," wrote Pliny, "the very smell of it alone recovers and refreshes our spirits, as the taste stirs up our appetite for meat." To smell of Wild Thyme was believed to raise the spirits (and does it not?) and the vital energies, while the odor of Garlic preserved those who partook of it or carried it about with them from infection.

Nor need we peer back into the dim past for cooroboration. We all know persons who are affected for better or for worse by certain odours. A woman once told me that the smell of white Lilac revived her no matter how low she might feel in mind or body. My father was made actively ill by the scent of blossoming Ailanthus trees and he carried on a small but animated feud with a neighbor who had two in her garden and refused to part with them—quite unreasonably, thought my father. To me the smell of Clove Pinks is instantly reinvigorating, while that of Roses (the true old Rose scent such as is possessed by the lovely dark red

> Over and over again I have experienced the quieting influence of Rose scent upon a disturbed state of mind, feeling the troubled condition smoothing out before I realized that Roses were in the room, or near at hand.

Rose Étoile de Hollande) is invariably calming. Over and over again I have experienced the quieting influence of Rose scent upon a disturbed state of mind, feeling the troubled condition smoothing out before I realized that Roses were in the room, or near at hand. The soothing effects of Lavender preparations are well known, and certain flower odours have an opposite effect, causing headache or nausea, even to the point of catastrophe, especially in a close room.

Miss Rohde ("Old English Gardening Books") quotes from the writings of a Dutchman who traveled in England in 1560. He wrote of the English people that "their chambers and parlours strawed over with sweet herbes refreshed mee; their nosegays finely intermingled with sundry sorts of fragraunte floures, in their bed-chambers and privy rooms, with comfortable smell cheered me up, and entirely delyghted all my senses." Perhaps we do not realize that so fragile and subtle an influence as a pleasant fragrance in our living rooms and gardens has the power to cheer us up and delight all our senses. But it is true. "For smell often operates powerfully not only in surreptitiously enriching and invigorating the mental impression of an event but also in directing the flow of ideas into some particular channel independent of the will." ["Aromatics and the Soul," McKenzie.]

But the subject is full of indistinctness, for a perfume that is a delight to one individual may be a horror to another. Memory, imagination, sentiment, a weak or strong stomach, are inextricably involved in our reactions. But do not many of us know from experience that a chance whiff from a hayfield, a Pine grove, the wayside bramble, the sea, often changes the mood of a whole day? A very old man once told me that whenever he smelled freshly sawed wood he felt instantly young and vigorous for a time. His youth had been passed in a New England village where there was a large saw mill and the acrid odor of fresh-cut wood was so strongly associated in his mind with youth and its abounding energy that it affected him physically.

Of course some persons are far more sensitive to such influences than others. Some there are, sadly enough, who are partially, or totally, anosmic, or nose blind, and to these a whole world of sensation and experience is closed. But there is undoubtedly a close and intimate connection between the sense of smell and the nerve centers and it is probably not fully understood how far reaching and profound is the influence of odour upon our mental state and physical makeup. Montaigne wrote:

> Physicians might in mine opinion draw more use and good from odours than the doe. For myself have often perceived that according unto their strength and qualitie, they change and alter and move my spirits and worke strange effects in me which make approve the common saying that the invention of insense and perfumes, in churches, so ancient and so far dispersed throughout all nations and religions, had a special regard to rejoice, to comfort, to quicken, to rouse, and to purify the senses, so that we might be the apter and readier into contemplation.

> A very old man once told me that whenever he smelled freshly sawed wood he felt instantly young and vigorous for a time.

In early times living-rooms, banqueting halls, churches and police courts were strewn with sweet scented herbs and flowers to disguise the odours rising from filthy and unsanity conditions, and dandies and great ladies hung about their necks gold and silver filigree baubles filled with fragrant gums to preserve their delicate nostrils from the vile effluvia arising from the piles of garbage and filth rotting in the streets. To-day we are proud of our sanity conditions but are not our noses assaulted by almost as vile effluvia, the reek of gasoline and oil that pollutes the air of our cities and even rises triumphant above the delicate scents of the countryside? Perhaps it may again become fashionable to carry about with us little perforated balls of gold or silver filled with precious sweet smelling gums and resins to offset the unpleasant olfactory contacts that assail us. . . .

The gardens of my youth were fragrant gardens and it is their sweetness rather than their patterns or their furnishings that I now most clearly recall. My mother's Rose garden in Maryland was famous in that countryside and in the nearby city, for many shared its bounty. In it grew the most fragrant Roses, not only great bushes of Provence, Damask and Gallica Roses, but a collection of the finest Teas and Noisettes of the day. Maréchel Niel, Lamarque and Glorie de Dijon climbed high on trellises against the stone of the old house and looked in at the second-story windows. I remember that some sort of much coveted distinction was conferred upon the child finding the first long golden bud of Maréchel Niel. Once a week, on Friday, a great hamper of freshly cut roses was loaded into the back of the "yellow wagon"—its physical aspect in no way bore out its sprightly name—and with "old Tom" in the driver's seat we fared into the city and distributed to the sick, the sad and the disgruntled, great bunches of dewy fragrant roses. . . .

The Box bushes grew tall in my grandfather's garden in Massachusetts, which has been little changed in outline for more than a hundred years. Their sharp scent seemed to bring about a special atmosphere of apartness and mystery, and when mingled with the simpler scents of herbs and the old time Roses, after a shower or an early frost, the odours of this lovely old garden would be raised to such a pitch of oriental richness that one felt transported straight out of green and white New England to the glamorous East. And to a small person creeping through the white gate to play, the usual game of young matron tidily keeping house beneath the Grape vine and competently managing a large family of dolls, seemed no longer fitting. Instead a distraught lady out of the Arabian

Nights glided with lissome grace up and down the straight paths, a fantastic head dress of Hollyhocks masking pigtails, a Lily scepter in her hand. . . .

Why do garden makers of to-day so seldom deliberately plan for fragrance? Undoubtedly gardens of early times were sweeter than ours. The green enclosures of Elizabethan days evidently overflowed with fragrant flowers and the little beds in which they were confined were greatly edged with some sweet-leaved plant— Thyme, Germander, Lavender, Rosemary, cut to a formal line. The yellowed pages of ancient works on gardening seem to give off the scents of the beloved old favourites—Gilliflower, Stock, Sweet Rocket, Wallflower, white Violet. Fragrance, by the wise old gardeners of those days, was valued as much as if not more than other attributes. Bacon said immortal things about sweet scented flowers in his essay, "Of Gardens," as well as in his less known curious old "Naturall Historie." Theophrastus devoted a portion of his Inquiry Into Plants to odours, chiefly floral and leaf odours. Our books of to-day make sadly little of the subject.

Our great-grandmothers prized more highly than any other what they called their posy flowers, Moss Rose, Southernwood, Bergamot, Marigold, and the like. Indeed it would seem that save in that strangely tasteless period of the nineteenth century, when all grace departed from gardens and hard hued flowers were laid down upon the patient earth in lines and circles of crude color like Berlin wool-work, Geranium, Calceolaria, Lobelia, and again Geranium, Calceolaria, Lobelia, no period has been so unmindful of fragrance in the garden as this in which we are now living. We have juggled the Sweet Pea into the last word in hues and furbelows, and all but lost its sweetness; we have been careless of the Rose's scent, and have made of the wistful Mignonette a stolid and inodorous wedge of vulgarity. We plan meticulously for color harmony and a sequence of bloom, but who goes deliberately about planning for a succession of sweet scents during every week of the growing year?

In England I have seen more than one scented garden. These were usually very charming and well carried out, a square or rectangular enclosure bound about with sweet-leaved briers, or a hedge of Box or Yew. Paved paths,

Philippe Mercier (1744-1747), *The Sense of Smell*, via Wikimedia Commons

the joints of which bulged with Thymes and low-growing Mints, separated the little beds in which grew all manner of plants with sweet scented flowers or leaves. And there was always a comfortable seat, for the English plan to sit and enjoy their gardens; they are seldom merely for interest or display. And a fragrant garden especially invites the sitter. One might quite happily make a gathering of fragrant plants on either side of a winding path. Here would be space for great bushes of Magnolias, Honeysuckles, Lilacs, Mock Oranges, bush Roses, all manner of sweet scented herbaceous plants and annuals, and along the verges broad patches of low-growing things, sweet Violets, Mignonette, Lily-of-the-Valley, Cowslips, Sweet Woodruff, with Clematis scrambling into the trees and other climbers supported on posts.

But interesting as collections always are to the collector and to those of like mind, it is more generally satisfactory to grow the sweet scented plants throughout the garden, as many as may be found room for, a precious leaven for the whole, and with special attention paid to those with sweet smelling leaves, for those are delightful for use in making nosegays.

A few agreeably scented foliage plants that should be grown in gardens for use in bouquets are the following:

Apple Mint	Micromeria	Basil	Old Woman
Bay	Orange Mint	Bergamot	Rose Geranium (tender)
Cedronella triphylla (tender)	Rosemary (tender)	Lavender	Southernwood
Lemon Geranium (tender)	Sweet Marjoram	Thymes	Lemon Verbena (tender)

For the most part fragrant flowers are light in colour or white. Brilliant flowers are seldom scented, though now and again there is an exception to prove the rule. There are more white scented flowers than any others and perhaps the purples and mauves come next. Some of the sweetest scented flowers are dull in colour, brownish or a sad purple. Flowers of thick texture are often heavily scented—the Magnolias for instance, Gardenias and those of the Citrus tribe. . . .

Gardens are sweetest when the air is mild and full of moisture. In periods of extreme drought and heat it will be noticeable that the fragrant ethers are appreciably lessened. Frosts, too, sets free latent fragrance, as does a shower of rain in many cases. . . .

Especially should small gardens, I think, be full of sweet scented flowers; it gives them a lovable intimate quality. And then if one thinks again, is it not just such endowment that a large garden has crying need of to make it more personal, more possessed, less aloof? One June 10, 1795, Horace Walpole wrote from Strawberry Hill, at "Eleven at Night":

I am just come out of the garden on the most oriental of all evenings, and from breathing odours beyond those of Araby. The Acacias, which the Arabians have the sense to worship, are covered with blossoms, the Honeysuckles dangle from every tree in festoons, the Seringas are thickets of sweets, and the new cut hay in the field tempers the balmy gales with simple freshness.

Poets have ever known how to turn to gentle remedial things in times of stress, to draw from simple sources healing balms and assuagements. The scents of flowers and leaves are without doubt among the most potent sources of such alleviation. In Mary Webb's lovely book, "Poems and the Spring of Joy," she puts it beautifully:

A thousand homely plants send out their oils and resins from the still places where they are in touch with vast forces, to heal men of their foulness. They link the places that humanity has made chokingly dusty with the life-giving airs of ambrosial meadows—bringing women's heads round quickly and setting people smiling.

Excerpt from *The Fragrant Path*, Louise Beebe Wilder (1878-1938). Originally published in New York by The Macmillan Company, 1932. In American gardening literature, the period of the late twentieth century is seen as a time when writers on this continent came into their own. Wilder was at the forefront in this genre and is recognized as one of the best English writers on the subject. In addition to this seminal book on how plant fragrance brings an amazing dimension of richness into our gardens, Wilder also wrote nine other books, including *Adventures with Hardy Bulbs, Colour in my Garden, Problems and Pleasures of a Rock Garden*, and *Adventures in a Suburban Garden*.

Looking for a few Green Men and Women.

(Because at **Greenwoman Magazine** we're on a mission!)

We created this magazine because we want to turn people on to art, to gardening, to saving Mother Earth, stuff like that. We think that those who are connected to these things can't help but live lives that contribute to a better planet.

If you'd like to help spread the word about our publication, we'd love to send you some back issues of **Greenwoman (our earlier, recycled paper version)** to share with your friends. Maybe at work, school, your garden club, community garden, book group, a Meetup group. . . there are so many possibilities!

Send us a note at sandra@greenwomanmagazine.com and let's get together to make the world a little greener. Thank you!

Logo design by Mike Beenenga

Euonymus Alatus

by Barbara Crooker

Outside my window, the bushes have turned, redder
than any fire, and the sky is the same blue Giotto
used for Mary's robes. My mother says if she still
had a house, she'd plant one or two of these bushes,
and I love how she's still thinking about gardening,
as if she were in the middle of the story, even though
we both know she's at the end. Down in the meadow,
the goldenrod's gone from cadmium yellow to a feathery
beige, the ghost of itself. Mother, too, fades away,
skin thin as the tissue stuffed up her sleeve.
The scars on her stomach itch and burn, but inside,
she's still the girl who loved to turn cartwheels, the woman
whose best days were on fairways and putting greens.
On television, we watch California go up in smoke,
flames leapfrogging ridge to ridge. Here, these leaves
release a shower of scarlet feathers, as everything starts
to let go. Oh, how this world burns and burns us,
yet we are not consumed.

(First published in *America.*)

Wikimedia Commons

Sex

in the

Garden

by

Elisabeth Kinsey

Illustration by Rachael Davis

(Mons) Venus in the Garden

I've always thought of Georgia O'Keeffe as the forward artist, blooming forth through flowers' wombs. But lately, I read on a friend's blog about a close-up photo of a woman's femaleness that distorts the image so that it's not apparent at first what you're staring at. While people sit in her office, it dawns on them halfway through the conversation what the image is. People usually ask, "Is that a . . . bush?"

I've had this same realization, but not so directly. I was driving along I-80 going east into Nebraska one afternoon, contemplating my impending divorce, when I saw little frizzes of rust or dark tangerine sticks jutting up during winter. As I passed the tufts of prairie grass, I thought, "Bush." In my mind's eye, I saw naked women lying with furry pubic bushes in contrast to the snow. This is when I conceived of having a sex garden, to regain my ego when I bought my new house.

I joked like a pubescent teen the day I bought my first house (first for the single me) that I would plant an X-rated garden. My divorce was final and I was untethered. The small house I bought from our settlement had a blank-slate backyard. The day I moved in, I wanted to celebrate and plan my garden all at the same time. What would be better than a divorce party/garden planning party with a handful of friends?

As my friends crowded my backyard (literally weeds and gnarly grass) I opened a bottle of wine and announced, "Let the sex gardening begin!" We snickered about what plants would align with the phallic, and then I hushed everyone: a vulva garden was what we needed. While we smoked (ahhh, the early thirties) and sipped, we made lists of anything that could be associated with bushes. "Girl power!" we yelled into the starry night, and surveyed the backyard for possibility.

The bush was so subjective; anything could be called a bush, even the mounds clinging to the ground. When we clinked glasses, my list included small shrubs, like horehound, oregano and mint, while one of my friends added furry lambs' ear and low-lying yet ever-blossoming asters. Also, we asked ourselves, "What can be groomed as a bush if let go to wander and get wiry?"

Many euphemisms flew that night such as, "I like my carpet to match the drapes (purple), so I'm planting Russian Sage." What started as a giddy foray into sex gardening ended up rising to our expectations. The Russian Sage grew up and out, bush-like. What Russian Sage does, much like prairie grasses growing along I-80, is advance to a quick, wild state, bristle upwards and flatten in a torrential downpour, only to spring back into action to border your garden in purple. Lavender won't grow up and out but will frizz around brick. Even though not a real bush, I picked the English type. The mounds of lavender go wild, and, like sex, they are a good thing you just can't have too much of. They're the perfect cut flower for when you prune (or shave it back). The scent will transform indoor spaces, pulsing perfume on a well-laid table.

I planted only perennials (Colorado, zone 5) so I would never look back. Plant once, enjoy the rewards year after year. Trim and shave at your own discretion. I added what most people think of when they think of a bush: an established purple lilac to block the view of the alley, a fire-bush (yes, there is such a thing, *Hamelia patens*, that by the end of the summer puts out red trumpets to capture any hummingbirds (a bird in the bush is . . .), and a variegated dogwood (because I had one at my ex's and I wanted it back).

Each bush wore out their welcome, except the lilac. I haven't pruned it in the "shaping" sense. I only took samples, year after year, to fill every vase I owned. The sweet scent reminded me of an expensive silk wrap, a flute of champagne on a perfect spring day. The dogwood I trim with a hedge trimmer, not to its roots but halfway back, and only in the fall. Every year, she asserts her presence on my front walk.

I tell some who come by, admiring my garden, how it started. It's how anything good begins, with a nice glass of wine, a little sex talk, and a garden dedicated to girl power: that is, power to the bush, or at least to the ones in my garden! ✿

Leafing Through
a review of books, etc.

*The Seed Underground:
A Growing Revolution to
Save Food*
by Janisse Ray
(Chelsea Green Publishing,
2012)

I bought this book on impulse. There was that charming cover with earthen bowls nestling beans and seeds and vegetables, with labels handwritten in pencil. It was April and the urge to put seeds in the ground had become overwhelming, even in the face of a sure spring blizzard and plummeting temperatures. The ground was not warm enough yet on the Front Range of the Colorado Rockies, so I decided to read about seeds rather than put them out too early.

It was an easy choice, as I admired the author, Janisse Ray. Her memoir, *Ecology of a Cracker Childhood*, published in 1999, opened my eyes to the dying ecosystems of longleaf pine forests that used to cover the Southeastern United States. Ray was able to merge personal narrative and environmental investigation into a tantalizing brew and rightly received plenty of critical attention for that first book. The *New York Times* declared: "The forests of the Southeast find their Rachel Carson." And I loved Janisse Ray's coming-home memoir, *Wild Card Quilt*, in which the author returns to her grandmother Beulah's farm and her childhood hometown to make a life with her young son after many years living far away from home. Ray's eye for destruction and despair is as unflinching as her determination to preserve a fading culture from extinction.

So reading her newest book, *The Seed Underground: A Growing Revolution to Save Food*, seemed just the thing to do as I waited for another early spring week to pass before the Front Range growing season began. She had me at the first sentence: "I am standing under the saddest oak tree that ever was." Ray prefaces the book with a young man's memorial service, the son of a friend who fell off a balcony to his death while partying with his buddies. As the funeral guests stand there sharing stories in the Florida Panhandle, an offshore rig explodes in the Gulf of Mexico, releasing millions of gallons of oil into the surrounding waters.

Ray drives home listening to bluegrass music on the radio and hears the lyric: What will you be building when you are called away? What she is building on her southeastern Georgia farm is what she calls "a quiet life of resistance," the life of "a radical peasant" growing as much of her own food as possible from seeds that have not yet been obliterated or supplanted by the genetically modified varieties that drive the corporate machinery of industrial agriculture in North America.

I have been reading about this stuff for years, ever since Monsanto started suing farmers for patent infringement when their GMO seed was transported by wind and germinated in unsuspecting, neighboring fields. When the heirloom tomato craze emerged a few years back, I grew some purple ones, barely understanding the concept of seed stock or how heirloom varieties were preserved over time. I have followed the growth of organics over the last decade and have watched with interest as people I know turned to saving and trading seeds.

But those people and those things have always seemed, somehow, beyond the reach of an urban gardener with a tiny backyard plot. I couldn't see what difference it really made if I grabbed any old packet of seed off the rack at Home Depot for my piddling plot of green beans, squash and tomatoes. If I wanted heirlooms or exotic varieties, I would rely on politically correct farmers in the Arkansas Valley to grow them and buy their vegetables at farmers market.

The beauty of *The Seed Underground*, recently tapped as a winner of the American Horticultural Society's 2013 Book Award, is that it takes all those conversations about big agriculture and the pioneers of the seed-saving movement and locally grown food and biodiversity, and it makes them as clear and simple as pushing a bean into freshly turned soil. "Seeds may be a small part of life," says Ray. "But they represent everything else. All our relations."

Ray makes it clear that we are losing our seeds fast in this country as well as our native plant wisdom. But she also offers clear information on how a home grower can take the first step toward "relearn[ing] the ancient wisdom of the wild garden" and "developing the heirlooms of the future" by saving and trading seeds. Or simply by buying seeds from companies that grow them with an intention of preserving biodiversity.

I learned more reading this book than I have in 25 years of backyard gardening. Now, it's time to get my hands dirty and get some seed in the ground.
—*Kathryn Eastburn*

Kiss My Aster: A Graphic Guide to Creating a Fantasic Yard Totally Tailored by You
by Amanda Thomsen
(Storey Publishing, 2012)

The title alone should clue you in pretty quickly that this is not your typical book about gardening and landscaping. Indeed, Amanda Thomsen's, *Kiss My Aster: A Graphic Guide to Creating a Fantastic Yard Totally Tailored by You*, is a novel approach to Landscaping 101. Most of the information is not necessarily new, but the presentation is quite unique, making it appealing for those who are looking for a book about gardening that is different, fun, and also informative.

Kiss My Aster is a graphic novel as well as a choose-your-own-adventure book. Each page features illustrations by Am I Collective that accompany her writing, and at the end of each section, the reader is presented with the option to skip ahead or back in the book depending on what they would like to learn. A common option is to skip to the section entitled, "Hire a Guy," for readers who may be feeling overwhelmed at any point in the process.

The scope of this book is broad, briefly covering all aspects of designing, constructing, and maintaining a landscape. The titles of each section are as amusing as the title of the book, including "Not Your Stepping Stone" which is about creating a stone pathway in your garden, "Drip It Good" concerning drip irrigation, "To B&B or Not to B&B" discussing the various ways that trees can be purchased (balled and burlapped, or not), and "Soil,

Yourself" which explains the inorganic components of soil. Games like Bingo, Word Find, and Mad Libs appear throughout the book in order to keep the wandering minds of readers entertained.

While the artwork is fun and the information is useful, the humor can be a bit distracting and over the top at times. Still, this book is meant to be useful while simultaneously entertaining, and it accomplishes both well. After all, where else are you going to find illustrations of pink unicorns and tips for warding off vampires while also learning about how to keep your lawn green without the use of synthetic chemicals?
—*Dan Murphy*

The Haunted Garden: Death and Transfiguration in the Folklore of Plants
by Sheryl Humphrey
(Sheryl Humphrey, 2012; available at www.hauntedgardenbook. tumbler-com)

"Now I shall tell of things that change, new being out of old..." –Ovid, *The Metamorphoses*, Invocation [Horace Gregory translation]

Some of us are drawn to the mysterious in horticulture—maybe it's carnivorous plants or sea-creature-like succulents that bring a thrill, or strange fruits and vegetables with surprising colors and unexpected tastes that surprise and delight. Some even enjoy a darker side of plant fascination. Perhaps they visit the saddest of gardens, cemeteries, and see the evergreens and willows, the antique roses, and lichen-covered statuary not as forlorn, but as bewitching and thought-provoking.

If this is you, and if you're a lover of mythology and legends to boot (we know who we are) this is a book you've been waiting for.

Sheryl Humphrey (a painter who beautifully incorporates the botanical and mysterious into her artwork) explores some of the plant world's most mesmerizing stories in *The Haunted Garden*. This self-published book is small (approx. 4" x 7") but brimming with tales of gods, goddesses, doomed lovers, twists of fate, creation, destruction, and resurrection. Apollo and Daphne, Echo and Narcissus and others are there, joined by Hindu legends, Native American and Scottish folklore, stories from The

Bible, and more.

Through tales of transformation, you will learn that plants and humans have been seen throughout the history of humanity as deeply connected, if not as one; this is something we should keep in mind these days.

I also loved that Humphrey brought the book into the present, touching upon ecology-minded "green" burials and the dangers of GMOs.

Educational and enchanting, this is the perfect book for an autumn night, preferably with a fire blazing and the full moon shining.

—*Sandra Knauf*

[Ed. Note: For a sample story, see "A Pot of Basil," pg. 14, in this issue.]

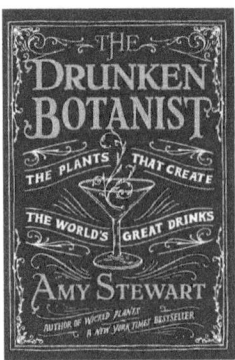

The Drunken Botanist: The Plants that Create the World's Great Drinks
by Amy Stewart
(Algonquin Books of Chapel Hill, 2013)

May I blame Amy Stewart for the slight drinking problem I enjoyed last year?

You see, I had never seriously pondered horticulture as it relates to the magic of alcoholic beverages. That is, until I started reading some of Stewart's articles about her book-in-the-making, *The Drunken Botanist*. In her blog *GardenRant* she shared some articles she'd written for the *North Coast Journal*. One was a mouth-watering tease about apples in alcoholic beverages (snappy hard ciders, tempting brandies, lip-smacking whiskies). Then there was the tasty post on her "Farmer's Market" drink, concocted with vodka, fresh tomatoes, celery, cucumber, peppers, cilantro or basil, and tonic water (muddle then steep while you finish garden chores), I also loved her glamorous piece on "literary" summer punches, a trio of recipes in homage to Annie Proulx, Jean Rhys, and Colette. I learned about exotic ingredients such as Lillet (a brand of French aperitif wine, 85% Bordeaux, blended with citrus liqueurs), Velvet Falernum (a liqueur with flavors of lime, almond, vanilla, ginger, and clove), and The King's Ginger (a ginger liqueur). How romantic it all was!

I became . . . curious (and curious for me often equals obsessed). It didn't help that a delightful new friend, writer Rebekah Shardy, happened to be a cocktail expert. At our first meeting, she wowed me with a beautiful and aromatic jasmine martini (vanilla vodka, jasmine extract, candied violet for garnish) and last fall she introduced me to a double espresso martini made with Kahlúa and Van Gogh brand (from Holland) double espresso vodka.

I, too, experimented. Last summer I tried a concoction of organic cucumber vodka, ginger beer, and St. Germain liqueur (made with elderflowers) that was divine. In March of this year I got to try a few beverages in Ireland—Bunratty mead (better than mead I've tried in the U.S.), Guinness (On tap! It's true what they say!) and "scrumpy" (a hard apple cider of which the farm-made version is infamous in Britain). With all this experimentation, I grew bigger while my pocketbook grew slimmer.

Then, Stewart's book came out. The book's design alone is cause for high praise (fonts, color scheme, gorgeous layouts and illustrations—Rebekah and I, meeting over nonalcoholic coffee one day, went ga ga over it) but its contents are what counts.

While there are plenty of recipes, *The Drunken Botanist* is mostly about botany, and is it comprehensive! You will be fascinated studying the processes of fermentation and distillation, and learning about the history of the grains, fruit, herbs, spices, flowers, trees, nuts and seeds that have undergone tipsy transformations. Stewart includes with some plants "Grow your Own" pages that explain how to do just that in your own garden.

The expansion of your cultural-horticultural knowledge alone is worth the price of admission. For example, were you aware that the plant that turns up most in alcoholic drinks worldwide is not barley, not grapes, but sorghum? Or how about the tidbit that sugar beets comprise 55% of the sugar produced in the United States? And since all commercial alcohol starts with a mix of cane and beet molasses to raise yeast, all commercial alcohol, therefore, starts, in part, with sugar beets? While Stewart is certainly a connoisseur, and always suggests the finest (often organic) ingredients, I wish she would have mentioned that the vast majority of sugar beets grown in the U.S. are GMOs; something that was eye-opening to me.

In Part Three of *The Drunken Botanist*, Stewart writes that "A thousand cocktails can be mixed from a kitchen garden." After reading Parts One and Two of this 380-plus page book, you will not doubt this. Part Three is the gardening section and there are ample "Growing Notes" on the plants that you can produce to create your own drinks, or drink embellishments.

I recommend this comprehensive work highly, for yourself or a mixologist friend, as *The Drunken Botanist* will be a useful and entertaining treasure for years to come.

—*Sandra Knauf*

Slow Flowers: Four Seasons of Locally Grown Bouquets from the Garden, Meadow and Farm
by Debra Prinzing
(St. Lynn's Press, 2013)

". . . sweet flowers are slow . . ."—*William Shakespeare*

The author and co-creator of *The 50 Mile Bouquet* (reviewed last year) returns with the results of an experiment: after writing about locally-grown flowers, Debra Prinzing wondered if it would be possible to create a local bouquet-a-week for her home. She put this to the test, using sources that included her own and friends' gardens, the wild, and flower farms.

Prinzing admits that at first she wasn't sure if she could meet the challenge—after all, she was a journalist, not a floral designer. However, she reasoned, she did have a journalist's passion for soaking up others' experiences. (I would add she also possesses an artist's eye, excellent local sources, a healthy budget for bloom buying, and, most importantly, the American can-do attitude.)

This book is the inspiring result of those 52 weeks, chronicled with Prinzing's well-wrought prose and her photography.

The arrangements are gorgeous, from the red and yellow tulips embellished with curly willow and budding *Camellia japonica* (the camellia from Prinzing's garden), to the flowering kale and tricolored sage of an understated autumn bouquet. While the majority of the blossoms, berries, branches, and even sedum were grown by professionals, we see arrangements made from the author's daffodils and summer snowflake (*Leucojum aestivum*), mock orange, bachelor's buttons, *Artemesia absinthium*, lady's mantle, peonies, and more. She also uses her own vases and containers, many of which are vintage American pottery (she writes a bit about that, too). The book is sprinkled with excellent tips on caring for and arranging cut ornamentals, with a separate section titled "Earth-Friendly Floral Techniques."

I had a great time admiring these seasonal bouquets and learning how they were put together, but it would be difficult for the average gardener to get the same results shown in this book. Prinzing has been a gardener for decades (and has, I'm guessing, a mature garden). Her home, in Seattle, is blessed with a mild climate and fertile soil, and locally-grown flowers are now popular and abundant there. And let's not forget that flower budget. It would be more challenging for the rest of us to duplicate Prinzing's experiment, but that's not the point. The point is about *possibility*—and the author, on that note, delivers a beautiful, fragrant, useful, and inspiring message.
—*Sandra Knauf*

Mother and Father Nature work on design concepts

Top Dressing

Lately Blooming by Cheryl Conklin

"I've just entered the final third of my life . . . I had expected to feel depressed, defeated, a sense of desperate urgency. Instead, I'm delighted."

I've just turned sixty, and I've developed an unexpected sensitivity.

I wish I could say that I am now able to detect cosmic messages in twigs fallen on the lawn. Wouldn't that be fun?

No, although somewhat mystifying, this is a sensitivity to certain phrases about age.

When I say, "I've just turned sixty," to someone who is, maybe, sixty-seven or eighty-two, I'm aware of how ridiculously young sixty sounds. It's a bit like being an initiate to a club that meets in a mythical garden.

In the other ear, when someone thirty-six or fifty-five sheepishly refers to herself as a late bloomer, I sense a pulsation between us. Call it what you will. Call it angst. Call it unsettled. Call it compelled.

There is something calling. Some dream. Some potential. Maybe greatness. Who knows?

Take it from a kindred "latester." In pursuit of authenticity, I writhed like an unpoled beanstalk through adulthood.

Ten years after I left college, for a homesteader's life in Northern Minnesota, one of my former professors convinced me to earn the final credit for my diploma. The only thing I ever propagated from it was entry to grad school.

Oh, I know! I'll become an art therapist.

At thirty-seven I finished the master's degree. Still, I didn't cultivate a field, let alone a sensible career.

I woke up one morning and wanted to garden. I was forty-seven and starting a gardening business. Despite success, true ambition was blasted in the bud.

I wrote a book and never even looked for a publisher. I didn't manage to have children. I didn't buy my first home until I was fifty-seven. Without a windfall, I will never pay off the mortgage.

Then, I turned sixty.

I've just entered the final third of my life. The leaves are quickly falling from the calendar. I had expected to feel depressed, defeated, a sense of desperate urgency. Instead, I'm delighted.

Like a plant informed by day length and soil conditions, all the signals confirm: This is my time. This is my true shape, and these are my true colors. I was born to have creases in my face and hair the shades of ashy bark. I've been waiting my whole life for the person now in the mirror. So has the world.

Some years ago, I planted a clutch of *Lilium speciosum alba*. Since her first appearance, she has become the most anticipated bloom of every season. Her buds swell in September. Such a pure and fragrant pleasure, the later she opens, the better. And although she may flower for weeks, well into October, she is always complete before a freeze. Such is her wisdom.

All this time, she was saying to me, "Just wait. You'll see."

Now, I've turned sixty, I've developed an unexpected sensitivity. I hear her. ❀